HEART-THROB

BY
MEREDITH WEBBER

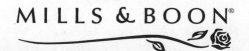

MILLS & BOON®

First published in Great Britain 1999
Large Print edition 2000
Harlequin Mills & Boon Limited,
Eton House, 18-24 Paradise Road,
Richmond, Surrey TW9 1SR

© Meredith Webber 1999

ISBN 0 263 16216 8

Set in Times Roman 16½ on 18 pt.
17-0001-49299

Printed and bound in Great Britain
by Antony Rowe Ltd, Chippenham, Wiltshire

CHAPTER ONE

Two days off and a sound night's sleep had promoted a feeling of well-being in Dr Peter Jackson's body, and filled his mind with a rare sense of goodwill to all men—and most women. Six o'clock, sign-on time, dawn breaking in an autumn sky, quiet reigning for once, accidents still waiting to happen. Even the sight of the poster adorning the wall of the emergency room, announcing him as Huntley Hospital's 'Heart-throb of the Month', failed to provoke his anger.

In fact, he smiled and eyed the slim, straight back of the woman studying it, admired the way her vivid red hair waved and frothed around her shoulders, slid his gaze downward to shapely calves and well-defined ankles— yes, he was definitely an ankle man!

Moved quietly closer.

'It's no good hankering after him, handsome though he is with that dark unruly hair and lethal grey-green eyes,' he murmured at the stranger's back. 'He's taken vows against matrimony, though not of celibacy, if you're at all interested.'

She whipped around to face him—eyes so blue he thought the sky had fallen—took one look at his face and swung back to his image, before turning again, slowly this time, and putting out her hand.

'I'm Anna Crane,' she said. 'Your new "team".'

He took the hand and shook it because his mother had brought him up with good manners, then he peered at her, trying to fit his mental image to the reality. She was tall—nearly as tall as he at five eleven—although she was cheating a little with short stubby heels on her shoes.

'Team, huh? I guess you've had a pep talk from our CEO. Rod's into Americanisms, in case you hadn't noticed, though why Americanising our accident and emergency department to an emergency room because of a TV show, should raise the profile of the hospital, I've no idea. And our "team"—that's you and me—still works a minimum twelve-hour shift no matter what we're called. You'll learn to be thankful for the quality nurses we have down here in the nether world of the hospital.'

He was blathering on a bit, mainly because he wasn't sure she *was* Dr Anna Crane—not the one he'd seen at the interview—although a badge pinned to her shirt, quite close to generous breasts, proclaimed she was who she said she was and also showed a photo that looked like her. The 'her' in front of him, not his memory of her.

The well-being was vanishing fast and goodwill fading to a memory as an unfamiliar confusion pricked along his nerves.

'Look,' he muttered, hating confusion in what he considered 'his' domain, 'I know I slept through your interview and for that I do apologise, but did you look the same as this back then?'

She smiled, the blue eyes crinkling at the corners in a most enticing fashion.

'I was wondering the same about you when I looked at the poster. It's the hair with both of us. You had a lot more on your face that day—designer stubble, isn't it called?' She put up her hand and frothed the pinky-red mass spraying around her head. 'As for me, the kids insisted I update my image before going back to work. I wasn't sure about the colour. I thought at first it was so bright it might frighten the patients, but I'm getting used to it.'

Kids! He remembered why he'd been against employing Dr Crane—the multi-married Dr Crane. She was currently single and no doubt on the prowl for husband number three. He'd worried her mind might be on marriage not medicine.

He shrugged, pretended the hair was just hair, ignored the fact that it must be the colour of it making her eyes look so blue and said coolly, 'I don't care if it's purple as long as you get the job done. Has someone showed you around—the doctor's office, the lounge room should any of us ever have time to lounge, the coffee-machine?'

She nodded in reply.

'I came in yesterday.' Blue eyes did the crinkling thing again as full lips curled into a rueful smile. 'I've been so terrified about coming back to work—so certain I'll have forgotten everything I ever learned—I spent the day following Paul and Jim around, probably getting in their way.'

He was about to say he didn't think she'd ever get in the way, but stopped himself in time. Such an inane comment from a man who abhorred inanities.

'Then come into the office and I'll introduce you to your desk—show you how to swear at the computers until they produce the info you need. By then the nursing staff should have finished their post-weekend gossip and be ready for parade.'

He led her past the reception counter, waving his hand towards Margie and saying, by way of introduction, 'Margie, Dr Crane—Dr Crane, Margie.' Margie had been responsible for the 'Heart-throb of the Month' nonsense and had to be treated coolly for a while. The problem was, none of the women with whom he worked so closely ever seemed to notice his cool. They were only too willing to reprimand him for his temper if ever he let fly, but ignored it completely when he tried to put them in their places with a dose of distant politeness. That was women for you!

'Margie does Outpatients Reception as well as our more acute admissions,' he explained to Anna, 'so she's flat out most of the time. When I'm on duty I have a nurse prioritise the emergency patients who walk in off the street— blood before bones, breathing before blood. It's very basic triage but it doesn't always work so you have to be alert when you're calling patients in or choosing who to see next.'

'If someone's slumped to the floor, pull him in before the sore toe?'

He glanced at her, certain she was laughing at him, but her lips were still and her eyes steadfast.

'Spot on,' he agreed, and wondered why the morning, still unriven by the blare of an ambulance siren, should be losing its appeal.

'Hey, heart-throb! And how was your weekend?'

'Dirty, no doubt!'

'Don't ask him, he might tell us!'

The four nurses emerged from the tearoom, greeting him with far too much familiarity. He scowled at them, ignored the 'couldn't have scored' jibe from Wendy Ahern and introduced Dr Crane.

'It's Anna,' she said, shaking hands with each of the women. 'And I must admit it's four years since I've been in this situation so I hope you'll all keep an eye on me and prevent me making any major blunders.'

Reassuring noises from the nurses. Talk about women sticking together! He'd be ragged for weeks about the most minor of mistakes and here were these women promising to protect one of their own.

'It's time we had some male nurses down here,' he grumbled, ushering his new 'team' away from the chattering women and into the office.

Which wasn't such a good idea because when he leaned over her shoulder to show her the filing system on the computer, he couldn't help but smell her perfume and notice the cleft between her breasts. Is this how she'd hooked husbands number one and two—pretending she didn't know she was attractive in a very primal way? Her lush woman's body the lure, her calm unassuming manner nothing more than camouflage?

'OK, doctor needed—a broken toe, I'd say.' Wendy, on triage today, saved him with her call. 'Carol's taken the mother and child into room one. If you want to take it, Pete, I'll show Anna the stock cupboards.'

Time to take a stand against this feminine conspiracy.

'No, Dr Crane can take the toe. She'll learn more doing than watching.'

She seemed unfazed by his command. She simply rose from her chair, pulled a white coat from the briefcase she'd been carrying, shaking it so the creases miraculously disappeared, slung a stethoscope around her neck, tucked a pad and pencil in her pocket and walked out of the room. Chatting to Wendy about X-ray facilities.

He let her go, waited at least half a minute then followed to stand in the doorway of the small curtained-off 'room' and watch as she calmed the mother, urging her into a chair while listening attentively to the angry explanation.

'Kicking his brother, that's what he was doing. Serve him right, I said to him. I can't be running you around to hospitals at this hour of a Monday morning.'

Then she calmed the child with understanding and empathy.

'It really hurts, I know it does.' His new 'team' examined the boy's foot as she spoke. 'I did the same thing myself when I was about your size, but I tripped going down the stairs. I couldn't tell anyone because I wasn't supposed to be out of bed—I just limped around until it got better.'

And your parents didn't notice? Pete thought, cynicism adding another layer to his doubt about this woman.

Yet she splinted and bound the toe with professional expertise, advised rest and elevation and paracetamol for pain. Much as he'd have done—but, then, any one of the nursing staff could have handled a broken toe so he'd reserve judgement.

'Asthma case in four, an infant who's inhaled a bead in three,' Wendy announced.

'Got a preference?' he asked, as Anna said goodbye to the child and his mother and saw them out of the cubicle.

'You choose,' she suggested, and he wondered, for an instant, which she'd prefer—decided the asthma so he gave her the infant. Later on he'd try to work out why.

He crossed the space between the partitioned-off 'cubicles' on one side of the big room and those on the other side. Part of the new 'grand plan' for the hospital included modernising the emergency department so the cubicles became real rooms where patients could be treated in more privacy. The board had wanted to do it the previous year, but Pete had argued against it, saying the money would be better spent on two well-equipped trauma rooms where critical 'first-hour' care could be provided.

He'd won that battle and the two rooms were a source of great pride to him, as well as necessary adjuncts to patient care.

The patients who needed minor procedures performed, or would simply be admitted to a ward, could wait a little longer for their privacy. In the meantime, when he was on duty the curtained 'rooms' were allotted in such a way it was only on the busiest of days that adjacent cubicles were occupied.

Joanne was with the patient—a young woman, cyanotic about the lips, who was breathing humidified oxygen through a mask held over her mouth and nose while trying to answer her admission questions.

'Yes, I think it was the hay. No, no problems with medications that I know of. No, I haven't been on steroids, no cold or other infection, no stress—it had to be the hay.'

He waited until Joanne had completed the list he kept for patients with any form of bronchospasm then stepped forward, took the chart and smiled at the patient.

'Hi, Sandy, I'm Pete. We'll get you sorted out as quickly as we can. Just a few more questions. When did this start? Did it come on slowly or suddenly?'

Sandy removed the mask to smile at him, returned it while she flirted a little over the top of it—brown eyes full of come-hither messages—then removed it again to speak.

'It started last night. I was at a bush dance put on by the local Scout group and they had these hay bales everywhere. I'm not usually this allergic to hay—I mean, I take my puffer with me and have a bit of Ventolin, and don't worry about it—but last night I just got worse and worse. In the end I went home and went to bed, thinking it would get better, but it didn't.'

'What else did they have apart from hay bales?'

Sandy looked surprised. 'Bush-dance kind of stuff—farm stuff, saddles and bridles hung around the place, branches of trees tied against the wall with stuffed animals, koalas and possums, in the branches.'

'Are you allergic to horses?'

'There weren't any horses. Yes, they do affect me but I'd have noticed if there was a horse.' She grinned at him, flirting again.

'Bridles and saddles will carry horse hair. Added to the hay, it probably triggered the attack. Now, according to your notes, you've suffered from asthma for as long as you can remember. How would you rate this attack?'

'As in bad, real bad or totally out of control?' she asked, and he nodded, smiling at the ratings.

She thought for a minute, breathed in more oxygen then removed the mask long enough to say, 'Between bad and real bad.'

'And what usually works for you?' he persisted, knowing most acute asthmatics knew their medication regime better than the doctors who treated them.

'Bronkosol through the nebuliser,' she reported. 'Usually one dose does the trick but I had to stay in the A and E department for a few hours and have another dose one time.'

He handed her a peak-flow meter and asked her to blow into it, saw the weak reading of seventy litres per minute, counted her respiratory rate—thirty-two—and asked Joanne to get the drugs and nebuliser.

'Sit with her while she has it,' he said when Joanne returned, 'then give her a buzzer so she can summon help if she deteriorates. Do fifteen-minute obs yourself—breathing rate and expiratory flow rate notations.'

Wendy was already calling him to the next patient—abdominal pain in six—while relieved voices from inside number cubicle three suggested his assistant had successfully extricated the bead.

So why did he have a naggy feeling in his gut?

It couldn't be working with a woman—he did that all the time. In fact, he enjoyed working with women and had a feeling he'd be hap-

pier relying on a woman to get a job done—
right through to the end—than he would on
many men. Though he'd never voice this opinion in male company. What men needed was
more solidarity between them—like women
had!

He entered cubicle six, shook hands with the
patient Kim introduced as Albert Smith, then
read through the admission notes.

'Been sore for a while, has it?' he asked the
gnarled old man on the bed in front of him.

'Bloody sore, mate,' the man replied. 'Reckoned it'd go away if I ignored it so I did. Guess
I reckoned wrong.'

Pete palpated the distended abdomen, felt
the tightness of the man's belly and asked
about bowel habits.

'Regular, mate, regular—every day or two
without fail, though lately it's not been the full
load, if you know what I mean.' He glanced
towards Kim, as if embarrassed to be discussing such things in front of a woman, then
groaned as Pete's hands struck a tender spot.

'Have you had any trouble in the past? An
operation of any kind on your bowels?'

Albert shook his head.

Blast! Adhesions from old surgery could cause bowel obstruction but in fifty per cent of cases it was carcinoma. Not something he'd wish on this poor blighter—any poor blighter.

'Well, we'll soon sort out what's causing it,' he said heartily, while wondering for the forty-thousandth time if A and E medicine was really what he wanted to do. He saw the patients hurting, the broken bodies of accident victims, not the miracles of medicine as they left hospital healed—or at least patched up. 'Kim's going to take some blood so we can find out what's happening there, then she'll wheel you through to X-Ray for a full set of pictures of your abdomen and I'll be back to put you on a drip. Any kind of obstruction will tend to dehydrate you so the sooner we get fluids into you the better.'

He left the cubicle, checked on his asthma patient, saw Dr Crane disappearing through the curtains around cubicle one and peered in.

She was leaning forward, talking earnestly to a woman who was seated on a chair beside the examination table. The patient's head was bent and she wept quietly, the bruises on her arms like vivid splotches of blue paint.

'I can put a small splint on it, tape it there and make sure there's no internal damage,' Anna was saying, crouching now so she could see the woman's face. She must have sensed his presence for she held up one hand as if to say, Stay still, don't interfere. 'As soon as the swelling goes down you'll at least be able to breathe. But if we leave it, and the septum heals crooked, you may never breathe properly again.'

'I can't go home with a plaster on my nose,' the patient cried. 'He'll know I've been somewhere, told someone.'

Pete felt his gut wrench and contract—his own personal and sickening reaction to violence, to abuse of a woman. He wanted to storm into the room, demand the name of her assailant and shift her out of the abusive environment right now, this very minute, but again his assistant's hand warned him not to move.

'Do you have to go back?' Anna asked the woman, then she sat back on her heels and waited.

'It's Mum—she's sick and he hits her if I'm not there.'

Pete closed his eyes, ignored the upraised hand and moved into the room, his stomach churning as he imagined the brutality this woman—and her mother—must have endured.

'I can get both of you into a special facility immediately,' he said, kneeling in front of the woman and taking her hands in his. 'It's a wonderful place, out in the country but not far from here. Your mother will be cared for, you'll be able to recover, and when you're both well you can decide what you want to do. I can send an ambulance for your mother right now. You have only to say the word.'

She looked up at him and he saw the swollen, reddened mess that had been her nose, the bruising coming out in purple streaks beneath her eyes, the puffy, tender upper lip. Bit his tongue to stop a swear word escaping.

'Perhaps it's time,' Anna said, stating a fact rather than adding a plea of her own.

The woman hesitated.

'Mum won't go,' she whispered, 'and I can't leave her there.'

'Why won't she go?' Pete demanded, 'I'll—'

Anna touched his arm, silencing him. 'Is your father at home today?'

The woman shook her head. 'He's gone fishing with his mates. Won't be back until tomorrow.'

'And how long have they been married, your parents?'

'Thirty-two years.' There was a pause, then she added, 'Thirty-two years of hell.'

'Thirty-two years ago there were no shelters for battered women—or not as many as there are today,' Anna said. 'People made a commitment to marriage and believed they had to stay within it—which was a good belief in ninety per cent of cases. Unfortunately, in the other ten per cent they should have got out.

'Your mother didn't and, having stayed this long, she feels it's no use trying to get away now. Maybe she thinks he's not as bad as he used to be—you probably hide the fact he beats you—or she's too tired and sick to bother about it. What if I go out after work and have a talk to her? Can she look after herself during the day if you don't go back?'

Pete saw the patient nod, but he was wondering about a twice-married woman giving

lectures on commitment. Still, she wasn't doing too badly with this particular patient so he
kept quiet.

'I can say I've admitted you to hospital, and
called to see if she was managing. I'll explain
that I can admit her, too, so she can be looked
after. You might find, if she's given the choice
of staying in the house without you or moving
somewhere safe, she'll choose to move.'

'And if she doesn't?' the woman asked.

That's the question, Pete acknowledged silently, watching Anna to see how she'd field
that one—seeing a tremor on her face which
suggested that the question had a deeper sig-
nificance.

'You have to decide what you'll do,' she
said. 'It's up to you. You're young and you
have years ahead of you which could be plea-
surable and fulfilling. All you can do is offer
your mother the chance to go with you, try to
persuade her that life can be better than it is at
present.'

'She won't come,' the woman said. 'I can
tell you that right now. She'll say he needs
her.'

As a punching bag? Pete thought, but he'd heard it all too many times, patched up too many broken noses, to be surprised. What did surprise him was Anna's attitude. Not that she should be offering to do house calls or taking on tasks probably better handled by the staff social worker, but—

'Well, let's fix your nose,' she said briskly as if the previous conversation hadn't happened. 'At least you can wear the plaster until your father comes home. That might help.'

Pete went back to insert a catheter for Albert's drip, saw a new patient brought in with abdominal pains—funny how things happened in clusters like that—sent him straight upstairs for an appendectomy, then heard the low whooping noise of the emergency alarm which always heralded trouble.

'A group of firefighters all with smoke inhalation problems, some with burns, three ambulances, seven or eight men—the driver who radioed in wasn't certain. Bushfire blew back on them.'

Pete turned to the nurses who'd gathered to the call, including two from Outpatients on the other side of the waiting room.

'OK, gang, break out oxygen in every empty cubicle, nasotracheal tubes, sterile dressings—keep the wounds dry until I've assessed them—and sterile water and Silvadene for minor burns. We'll run IV lines into anyone with second- or third-degree burns and patch up first-degree. Remember smoke inhalation can impair the lungs and patients could end up with adult respiratory distress syndrome if not carefully observed so if there's any doubt about their lungs we'll X-ray.

'I want everyone in scrubs—sterile conditions. No matter how blackened and ash-scattering our patients might be, we don't want to introduce any hospital-generated bacteria into their wounds.'

He dismissed them all to pull on sterile clothing and prepare cubicles. He saw Anna move off with the nurses and caught up with her.

'Where's your patient? Is she willing to be admitted?'

She shook her head, the red hair rippling around her face, reflections of it making the pale skin seem illuminated from within.

'Not admitted, but I've persuaded her to stay here until I finish work. She's happy to go outside and lie on the grass in the sun for a while. I don't think she gets a lot of time to smell the roses.'

A wistful note in her voice made him study her more closely, but she met his eyes and smiled guilelessly. Not a lot to read there!

Not a lot of time. The ambulances screamed into the drive and the rattle of wheels told him gurneys were already rolling.

It was an exercise they'd all experienced, even Anna, he realised as he poked his head into a cubicle later to see her intubating a patient with a skill and dexterity he'd admire one day when he had more time.

Albert was dispatched to Men's Surgical after ultrasound revealed a mass in his large intestine below the compacted faeces and Pete returned to the worst of the burn victims. Fluid was running into the man's arms through two wide-bore catheters, morphine had been administered in the IV line to ease his pain, his wounds were loosely covered with sterile dressings, he was intubated and on oxygen. All they needed was the orderly from the burns unit to arrive for the transfer.

Pete explained to the man, a senior fireman if the gold braid on his uniform was any indication, exactly what was happening, and saw the understanding in the man's eyes. All part of the job, he seemed to be saying. Pete remembered his rage when he'd seen the woman's bloodied nose and told himself that the same applied here.

'I think my patient should be transferred to the burns unit.' Anna's voice broke into his thoughts. 'The burns aren't serious—first to second degree—but they're on his hands and forearms and I feel there's a risk of circulatory compromise with the swelling. Would you admit?'

He nodded.

'Get him upstairs, then start on the other patients. Clean the wounds with sterile water and Betadine, cut the skin off large blisters, use Silvadene and an absorbent dressing. Don't let anyone go until you're satisfied they're breathing's stabilised—pulse and BP within normal range.'

She walked away from him, moving swiftly but without any indication of extreme haste or panic. Unflappable. He liked that in his emergency department, he admitted as he lifted the phone to tell the burns unit they were sending two patients, not one. Let them make the decision when to send the second man home.

She debrided blisters neatly, too, he decided, watching her at work a little later. In fact, if she went on like this he could stop watching and get on with his own job.

It was two o'clock before the rooms were cleared of firefighters, the asthmatic girl discharged and there were no emergencies demanding medical intervention. He found Anna pushing her disposable gown into a trash bag in cubicle four.

'Theoretically we go to lunch at different times, but if you'll make do with a sandwich and a cup of coffee we could go through to the lounge and combine lunch with a chat about how things work. Someone will find us if we're needed.'

She glanced at him then picked up her white coat and shrugged back into it.

'I brought my lunch,' she said, 'but coffee would be very welcome.'

He walked with her to the room, realising their steps matched—or that she was accommodating her stride to his. Did men ever do that to women? Did he?

He wasn't certain—rather thought he expected them to keep up as best they could. Perhaps not.

And why Anna Crane was making him think of men and women, he didn't quite know. Perhaps it was that perfume, so faint he might be imagining it—elusive, haunting.

Addictive?

Nonsense. Even if he had any intention of marrying, which he didn't, a twice-married woman would be the last person on his shopping list.

Yet he watched her covertly as she settled into one of the battered leather armchairs, sighed and pulled a packet of sandwiches out of her briefcase.

'Why the vows against matrimony?' she asked as she unwrapped her lunch, not looking at him, her voice so casual he knew she was simply making polite conversation. Though

how she'd honed straight on to his thoughts
was a mystery.

'I chose emergency medicine as a specialty
because I like the hustle and bustle, the adrenalin rush of it. But it's hardly suited to placid
domesticity. It involves such long working
hours, regular shifts of night duty, stress that
you don't always leave behind on the job.'

'Very rational thinking,' she said, lifting an
eyebrow and allowing a smile to tilt her lips
so he guessed she'd have liked to add, 'for a
man'. 'And your family, your parents? They
have no desire to see themselves perpetuated
in your children, no dynastic regrets that
you've opted for a single life?'

He looked up from the coffee he was pour-
ing. It was a strange question from a new acquaintance.

'They've five other children,' he explained.
'All busy breeding with vigour and enthusiasm. The survival of my parents' gene pool is
definitely ensured.'

'Six of you!' She breathed the words as if
it was a marvel of some kind. 'Were you a
happy family?'

He stopped to think.

'I think so. I know it's fashionable to suffer angst about one's childhood, but somehow I can never find anything more than minor incidents of great embarrassment in my past. Most of those during adolescence.'

She grinned at him. 'No angst?'

'None,' he admitted regretfully. 'You?'

And was immediately sorry, for the blueness seemed to fade from her eyes, leaving them a clouded-sky kind of grey.

'Oh, only one,' she said. 'One angst-invoking incident.'

She spoke lightly but he guessed it was a whopper so he didn't pursue it, not because he didn't want to know but because he was fairly certain she had no intention of telling him.

Not that it mattered. She'd be gone and another 'team' would be in place before he had time to turn around. Not many people lasted in a small department like this. Sometimes he wondered if it was only stubbornness which kept him here—stubbornness and the fact his sisters and brothers had stolen all the other specialties!

'How much of the paperwork do we transfer to the computer files?' she asked, her voice, soft but clear, recalling him to the reason they were eating together.

'Clerical staff will enter all the data from the patient's admission form and the form which comes with an ambulance patient. We can leave those spaces blank and go straight down to the space under ''Procedures'' and make a note of what we've done, treatment given. At this stage, you should check that it's all entered on the chart as well—or the copy of it which you retained if the patient's been admitted.

'It's also critical to document the instructions you gave the patient and his or her family about follow-up procedures—wound care, dressings, medication, when to come back for a check-up, whether or not the patient should see his or her GP.'

'Concerned about litigation?' she asked. One fine, pale eyebrow rose and her lips took on a teasing tilt.

He refused to be beguiled into smiling back at her, no matter how alluring that smile was.

'We should all be aware of the possibility and the ramifications any suit would have, not only on the hospital but on the local community. Plant a seed of doubt and it will flourish—'

'And the locals wouldn't come when they should—might delay treatment which could have helped them. Do you think a damages suit could have that much effect—especially when Huntley's the only public hospital in the area and most of the townspeople were probably born here?'

'I've read of incidences where it's happened,' he said, wondering about this woman who seemed inclined to go an extra step—in asking questions, pursuing answers, helping patients.

Was this first day 'making a big impression' stuff, or was she always interested in everything about her? Would she continue to take that extra step?

Probably not. He knew she was currently unattached—her CV had made that clear. He was willing to bet big dollars she was here to find husband number three. Perhaps that's why she'd questioned him about his intentions.

Well, he'd certainly made his position clear!

CHAPTER TWO

PETE had little time to think about Dr Anna Crane for the rest of the afternoon, with a trickle of domestic and work-related accidents coming steadily through the door.

'How's your young woman?' he asked her as they passed in the corridor between the cubicles at about five-thirty.

'She's still here—moved into the foyer when it grew cold outside, and she's waiting for me there.'

He wanted to tell her not to get involved, but he couldn't because he knew he'd probably have done the same himself. Although that was different, wasn't it?

'Well, at least you should get out of here on time,' he offered, then heard the wail of sirens. Kelly, the afternoon-shift receptionist, warned them to expect the victims of a pile-up on the freeway outside town.

Five patients—a family of four and the driver of the truck they'd hit, or been hit by.

The logistics of blame didn't matter when injured people came through the doors.

The late-shift nurses swung into action, passing out scrub suits, setting up the cubicles. The ambulance men would have prioritised the patients and Pete knew the first two through the door would go to the trauma rooms. Two adults, obviously the parents—presumably the driver and front seat passenger.

'Got to be internal bleeding,' the ambulance bearer said as he helped the orderly push the gurney carrying an injured man. 'His blood pressure was up at first but it's dropping fast. He was restrained by a seat belt and has seat-belt injuries, fractured rib and clavicle, by the feel of things, as well as a broken femur.'

Pete listened and looked, then made a quick decision.

'Jill, get on to Theatre and tell them I'm bringing this patient straight up. Probable aortic tear.'

Had to go with him in case he arrested on the way. He glanced at Anna who was walking beside the second gurney, steering it into the first trauma room.

Would she cope? Well, she'd have to. He'd be back in a few minutes, anyway.

On his return he found she'd not only coped, she'd done brilliantly. Blood had been despatched to Pathology for typing, a catheter had been inserted into the woman's subclavian vein and fluids were running in, the portable X-ray had confirmed a broken pelvis and, listening to Anna speak to a surgeon, Pete realised she suspected abdominal injury.

'Sending her straight upstairs?' he asked.

'Yes, they've a team waiting for her,' she replied, her fingers resting lightly on the woman's wrist, her attention on the patient not him. 'I won't leave the hospital until a relative has arrived to be with the children,' she promised the woman, then she nodded to the orderly who'd come down from Theatre.

'Do you know of a relative?' Pete protested. 'These people could be from interstate, travelling through from anywhere. You can't take on everyone's problems down here, and you shouldn't make promises you can't fulfil.'

She grinned at him.

'I'll try not to,' she assured him. 'But I do know this family is local—they were driving out to see the new house they're building on the other side of town when the car skidded on a greasy patch on the road—seems it's raining out there.'

'The woman was able to tell you all of this?' She looked surprised.

'Yes. She was woozy, of course, because after I'd checked for head injury I gave her some morphine for the pain. I did a peritoneal lavage and found blood in her abdomen but she was more concerned about the children than her health and wanted to know they were being looked after before she'd consent to surgery. Jill's contacted the patient's mother who should be here any minute.'

'And the children—have you checked on them?'

She frowned at him, as if his question was unnecessary.

'They're shaken, of course, and a little bruised, but both were in approved car-seats with safety harnesses on. They're fine.'

'Which leaves the truck driver.'

'He's in with the children. Seems he knows them—in fact, he's one of the carpenters working on the house. Badly bruised chest from his seat belt, but it appears he saw the car go out of control and guessed it would skid into him. He braked so the impact wasn't too bad, but because he knew the family he came in with them to see what he could do.'

Pete shook his head.

'Did you glean all this information while I went up in the lift to the third floor and back down again?'

Another cheeky smile, the blue eyes sparkling with a mischievous delight. 'People talk to me.' One shoulder lifted in a kind of shrug as if to say, I don't understand it either. 'It's one of the reasons I'm good in an A and E department.'

No pride in her voice but no false modesty either—simply stating a fact—and he couldn't argue with it if today was any indication. In fact, he wasn't quite sure what to say. He glanced at his watch. Six-fifty! Not a bad start to the week.

'Well, the new "team" is officially on duty. You're free to go. Hope you enjoyed your first day at Huntley.' It sounded lame but he was uncertain of himself around this woman, who'd not only displayed a competency he hadn't expected but exuded a subtle femininity he found disturbing.

'I'll stay until the children's grandmother arrives,' Anna said, moving towards the cubicle where the children would be waiting.

'But the truck driver's there and he knows them better than you do,' he argued. 'You're going to be late enough getting home, with your other patient and her mother to see to on the way.'

She peeled off the soft scrub suit she'd been wearing and shoved it in a bin, ignoring his comment, his advice.

Well, not entirely, for now she turned towards him. 'I told the mother I'd wait. It's the least I can do.'

You won't last, he wanted to say, but thought that too blunt so tried a softer tack.

'You can't take a personal interest in every patient who comes in here. You'll burn out too quickly.' She glanced at him and he saw something in her eyes, a steadfast purpose perhaps, but she didn't argue. 'You've obviously got an interest in and a gift with people so why come here where they flit past you? Shouldn't you be in general practice where some involvement in the patients' lives is necessary for efficient and effective medicine?'

'Why are you here, Dr Jackson?' she asked.

'Didn't you say it was for the hustle and the bustle, the challenge of it all?'

How dared she use his own words against him?

'Yes, but—'

'But women don't need that kind of challenge, that adrenalin rush you spoke of?'

'How do I know what women need?' he muttered pettishly, and was even more aggravated when she grinned at him and threw a glance towards the heart-throb poster.

He was going to tell her that it was all nonsense, a fund-raising idea leading up to the hospital fête, but she'd moved away and was hurrying to meet an anxious-looking woman. The children's grandmother? Did Anna Crane have ESP as well? Most people walking into this department looked anxious so how could she tell?

He turned back towards the cubicles and found the children, as she'd said, sitting one on each side of a tall, lean man with a bandage wrapped, pirate-fashion, around his head. All three seemed unperturbed by their brush with death, although the younger child, a little girl, began to cry when her grandmother appeared.

'Thank you for taking such good care of them,' the grandmother said to Anna, then she turned to Pete and began to ask questions about the parents' injuries.

'I'll be off,' Anna said quietly, and she slipped away. Needing to get on with her next Samaritan act or upset because she was seen as the care-giver and he the medical expert?

No, he certainly didn't know much about women for all the heart-throb tag. Although he understood his sisters, surely! Knew what made them tick.

He answered Mrs Granger's questions while his mind asked more of its own, totally unrelated to the moment or to the work in hand.

And was still asking them next morning when he returned to work to find his 'team' already there again, bright-eyed and bushy-tailed, while he'd slept badly and was grouchy, not up to bright at all!

She was also busy, working with one of the nurses to calm an obstreperous drunk while the night-shift doctor stitched his foot. The man had been sick and had possibly poured a bottle of rum over himself, judging from the smell, yet Anna seemed oblivious of it as she spoke quietly to the patient, explaining that he could go home after they'd dealt with the wound and offering to phone someone to come and get him.

A stream of abuse greeted this remark and Pete gave her a point for not flinching from it. He was about to intervene when a new patient demanded his attention—and hers.

'MI in trauma room one,' Margie called across the hall to him—apparently loud enough for Anna to hear for she followed him out of the room.

'I've got to get a better system organised for alerting the medical staff to patients,' he muttered, more to himself than Anna, as they walked into the small room where Kim was already noting down vital signs and Joanne was attaching electrocardiogram leads to the patient's arms, legs and chest.

Anna took the chart from Kim and passed it to him, picked up a nasal cannula and, after a swift glance at Pete for confirmation, explained to the patient what she as about to do. She lifted the oxygen mask the ambulance men had provided and slid the small tubes expertly into place, before reattaching the oxygen and adjusting the flow meter.

Pete was aware of her working beside him as he slipped a nitroglycerine tablet under Mr Grayson's tongue—that should start the blood vessels expanding while he dealt with the pain. Found a vein and inserted a catheter, morphine first, then fluid, more nitro later, slow infusion. As always the steps in reclaiming life repeated themselves in his head, the warnings following them.

'Do you use heparin or aspirin or both at this stage?' Anna asked, and he realised she was following the same steps in her mind, wondering about the possible side-effects of more aggressive drugs.

'Both,' he said, 'and restrict it to that until the patient's feeling more comfortable and can give us his medical history.'

She nodded.

'I once saw a patient who'd recently had two teeth removed given TPA and streptokinase,' she said. 'Talk about dissolving clots! The staff attending her had taken her medical history but she'd not mentioned teeth, assuming them to be non-medical.'

He shuddered, imagining how confused the patient's system must have been, receiving messages from the brain to form clots and messages from the drugs to dissolve them.

'Bad outcome?' he asked, and she nodded.

'Second heart attack as the heart tried desperately to pump more blood to her brain while it leaked out into her mouth. She did recover, but had a third infarct twelve months later.'

He didn't have to ask about the outcome of a third incident but asked Mr Grayson about his general health instead.

'So, no recent injury where you've been bruised or bled? No ulcer, history of bleeding?'

Mr Grayson, less pale and sweaty now the pain was easing, assured them he was a very fit and healthy man. Well, he might be just a trifle overweight but still...

Carol stuck her head around the door to call Anna to another patient, and Pete continued pumping chemicals into his, wanting him stabilised before he was despatched to the coronary care unit.

It was mid-afternoon before their paths crossed again—a lull in the patient flow, time for coffee taken sitting down instead of on the run.

'Given all the evidence on the harmful effects of drinking coffee, you'd think hospitals would have been the first places to dispense with these machines,' Anna remarked as she held up a cup and raised her brows in a silent query.

'Yes, please,' Pete answered. 'Black with two sugar, and if they took coffee machines out of hospitals the human machinery would grind to a halt. How else would we keep going, without our caffeine addiction?'

She smiled at him but said nothing. She simply passed him his cup and scttlcd down herself, once again pulling sandwiches out of her briefcase like a child retrieving her lunch from her school-bag.

'Does your mum make your lunch?' he teased, following the simile through.

She looked startled for a moment, then chuckled.

'No, this mum makes it. I make lunch each day for the kids although they object strenu-

ously, believing processed chips or sausage
rolls from the canteen are far cooler in the eyes
of their peers. I could hardly buy mine when
I won't let them buy theirs.'

'Not even on special occasions?' he asked,
remembering similar arguments with his own
mother over the advantages of school canteen
lunches.

'Once a week, Fridays,' she conceded, 'and
I refuse to ask what they spend their money
on because I don't want to know.'

They sounded like older children, from the
way she spoke, but surely she was too young.
He wanted to ask her but wasn't sure how.
Asked about her battered patient instead.

'How did you get on with the mother?'

She sipped her coffee, took another bite of
sandwich, chewed it thoroughly, then met his
eyes.

'Not well,' she admitted, 'but I live in hope.
I left them my number here and at home and
told Janice—that's the daughter—to phone me
if her mother seemed like weakening. I said
I'd organise things with the refuge and arrange
transport. Was it Crystal Creek you were considering?'

He nodded. 'Are you a local? I should have known that from your application but somehow—'

'It also put you to sleep,' she teased. 'I don't wonder after the workload you'd been carrying that weekend! No, I'm not local, but I've lived here for four years and while I wasn't working I did voluntary work at Crystal Creek.'

What was she? Wonderwoman? The perfect mother preparing lunches for her children— and how many could she possibly have? The ideal citizen doing charity work? What about her husband? Husbands, plural. Had they been left behind in this welter of goodness?

Irritation with her scratched along his skin but when she rose to answer the next call to a patient—add scrupulous in taking her turn to her good points—he wondered if the irritation might be with himself because he was interested in her.

And didn't want to be.

She was obviously the marrying kind, and he wasn't, so there was no point in starting something that couldn't be satisfactorily resolved for both parties.

Full stop.

He ignored her for the rest of the afternoon, well, as much as possible when they both worked in the same department. She was stitching up a child who'd fallen through a plate-glass window when six o'clock, and the end of shift, arrived. He poked his head into the cubicle.

'I've nearly done—you go,' she said to him. Taking over now?

Not really, he was just feeling aggravated—hadn't really recovered all day. He *would* go. What's more, he'd call in at the local and have a light beer—forget about Anna Crane.

His decision made, he said goodbye to the staff who were within sight, grabbed his brief-case containing some figures he wanted to review for the next staff meeting, and was on his way out the door as a shaggy-looking youth ambled in, followed by a young girl who by-passed him and went across to study the poster on the wall.

'Dr Crane around?' the young man asked, his dreadlocks moving listlessly as he swung his head to see if he could see her. Pete caught the glint of silver above his eye, saw the eyebrow ring and shuddered at this new mania for body-piercing among the young.

The girl returned, studying him as if to match his face to the poster—not all that difficult, he felt.

'She works here,' the lass added hopefully.

'She's busy,' he told the pair. 'Can I help you? I'm Peter Jackson. I'm a doctor here as well.'

'You're her boss?' the young man said, then he glanced at the girl. 'The heart-throb, Jackie.' Looked at Pete and added, 'Could we talk to you? Outside?'

Bemused by the invitation, Pete went, feeling almost guilty as they'd both looked surreptitiously around the room before herding him out the door.

'I'm Josh and this is Jackie. Josh and Jackie Crane, Anna's stepkids.'

Well, that solved one problem—she didn't have to be all that old to have stepchildren who argued about canteen lunches.

'We've had this idea, you see,' Jackie began, after they'd both shaken hands with him, 'and we thought it would be really easy once Anna started work, but now we realise that it

won't be as easy as we'd imagined. We're going to need help.'

Josh moved restlessly, perhaps realising
how little sense his sister was making.

'We want to get her married again,' he said
bluntly. 'After all, Jackie and I, we won't be
with her for ever. In fact, I'll be off to uni next
year and Jackie a few years after that.
Although we'll always come home, and she'll
always be special to us, we can't stay there for
ever. But, on the other hand, we don't want
her to have a lonely old age.'

Pete hid a grin. Did Anna realise this was
how the children saw her—tottering towards
old age? And a lonely one at that?

'Besides, she's still young enough to have
children of her own if we get moving and fix
her up pretty soon,' Jackie put in firmly. 'She's
a great mother and she really loves kids.'

'We thought when she got this job, well,
keen, she'll meet all kinds of men at the hospital. Then we realised, when she came home
yesterday and told us about it, that she wasn't
really getting out and about at the hospital, just
stuck down in the emergency department with

a bloke who doesn't want to get married anyway.'

Josh, who'd taken over the duet recital, blushed and stammered out an apology as soon as he realised what he'd said.

'I'm sure Dr Jackson understands what you mean.' Jackie rescued him. 'It wasn't that we expected her to meet someone straight away, or that we think she'd ever marry anyone she didn't fall in love with, but we realised we needed someone who could sort of introduce her around. Perhaps someone who's been here for a while and knows the staff, knows who's married and who isn't—that kind of thing.'

Pete shook his head in disbelief and looked from the unprepossessing owner of the dreadlocks to the gangly young girl, then back again.

'We don't want her getting into trouble,' Josh admitted, a worried frown scoring his forehead. 'I mean, she hasn't been around much at all and probably wouldn't know if a bloke's just after one thing—' He blushed again but went on manfully. 'Or interested in commitment.'

Twice married and this innocent kid thought she hadn't been around much? He kept his thoughts to himself as Jackie launched back into the persuasion.

'It's hard for us to find people to introduce her to. Then, when she mentioned you... Well, Josh always teases her so he started up and she told us what you'd said about not being into matrimony—and later on Josh and I were talking and we thought maybe you'd be willing to help.'

'You see, she told us about the heart-throb thing and how a different person is chosen each month, and we thought if you could make her a heart-throb for a month and her picture was all over the hospital—well, she's not that bad-looking, is she?'

Pete found his head moving from side to side again as if the shaking motion might clear the drowning sensation in his brain—drowning in a flood of words. Thought about protesting that matchmaking wasn't his forte, explaining that the heart-throbs were all men, but left it too late for Jackie was back in full flow.

'We'd leave it up to you to decide how you work it so if you don't think the heart-throb thing would take we'd go along with that.' She looked up into his face, melting, chocolate-brown eyes adding pathos to the plea. 'Would you help us? Would you? Please, please, please?'

This repetition must be an adolescent thing—he had a niece who always asked three times. Was three an optimal number? And why was he thinking about threes and adolescents when he should he extricating himself from any involvement with Anna Crane—particularly any involvement which included setting her up with husband number three?

Three again!

Although—

'I'll think about it, kids,' he said, as a conviction grew that marrying her off to someone else might be an excellent idea. He'd never lusted after other men's wives so, once she was safely hitched, he'd no longer feel an urge to skim his gaze across her ankles or watch the way her breasts moved as she walked. 'Seriously,' he added, as the idea became more appealing, 'I've got your phone number on Anna's personnel details so I'll phone you when I've got something sorted out.'

The two youngsters whooped with joy, Jackie going so far as to fling her arms around his neck and kiss him firmly on the cheek. He felt her warmth, smelt the slightly sweaty child-smell of her and told himself he was quite certain he didn't want children of his own. It was only occasionally he felt a nagging wonderment, a kind of inner questioning. How would he handle bringing up a child? What would a child of his be like—?

'Hi, kids, have you introduced yourselves to Dr Jackson?'

The warmth in Anna's voice told him she was as fond of her stepchildren as they must be of her, to be planning to fix her up so she wouldn't have a lonely old age. Grinned to himself as he pictured her shock and embarrassment if she learned the real reason for the pair's visit. Decided finding her a man might be fun.

Or plain daft!

It was two days later, Thursday, and Pete had set himself the task of getting Anna a date for Saturday night. Studied her personnel file to find her age and interests. Thirty and none

as far as the file went. Well, no sporting interest listed, no hobbies—if you didn't count
catching husbands—nothing to indicate which
of the bachelors he knew might click.

Decided the new chap up in O and G might
be looking for someone to show him the sights
of Huntley. According to his personnel file—
which some sweet talking down in Records
had produced—he was thirty-two and single.

Gay or just too busy to have found himself
a wife? Pete chided himself for the thought.
He was thirty-seven himself and single and rel-
ished his bachelorhood. Phoned through to O
and G, wondering what on earth one said when
setting up a blind date, got hold of Ken Riddell
and mumbled something about having a new
staff member in the emergency department and
thought it might be nice if a few other new
staff got together.

Realised he was organising a party!

Ken sounded so enthusiastic he wondered
why the hospital didn't think to put on a do of
some kind for all the staff early in the year
when all the 'newies' were still settling in. The
hospital ball was June—by then they'd been
floundering in a new social sea for six months.

'I'm having a few old and a few new staff at my place on Saturday evening,' he said to Anna when they met for a late-as-usual lunch during the two o'clock lull. 'Casual buffet kind of dinner, nothing fancy. Would you be able to come?'

She looked surprised, then puzzled—not particularly pleased, although he was going way beyond the call of duty and his commitment to her kids!

'I suppose so,' she replied doubtfully. 'Can I bring something? What dishes are you having? Will I do a casserole? Or something sweet? A pavlova and cream, fruit salad?'

He stared at her, puzzled by her reaction to the invitation.

'Do you only go places where you can bring something?' he asked.

The doubt dissolved into a cheery grin.

'I don't go places,' she told him. 'I guess that's why I was surprised. Also by your putting on a dinner for new staff—I mean, no one would expect you to go to that much trouble by yourself when it's so easy if everyone chips in.'

She came to a halt. Had she felt her words causing aggravation?

'Because I'm a man, or because I'm single, you wouldn't expect me to go to any trouble?' he demanded, then remembered what had made him mad in the first place. 'And why don't you go places? Have you taken some vow to remain faithful to your late husband's memory?'

He'd found out about her second husband's death from her files and didn't know whether to feel better or worse about her marriages.

'I'm sorry if I offended you,' she said slowly. 'Of course a man can prepare a meal as well as any woman—most of the world's great chefs are men.' A rueful grin. 'And probably single, given the hours they work. But if I can do anything to help, I'd be glad to,' she finished, neatly avoiding the 'going out' question and the comment about her husband.

Letting him know it was none of his business?

'Well, thanks for the offer but I'll manage,' he said, wondering what his cousin Liz would say when he asked her to cater the dinner at such short notice. 'Do you have my address?'

Stupid conversation. Of course she didn't have his address! He wrote it on the back on the paper napkin he'd picked up from the coffee-table and passed it to her, startled when she tore the address from the rest of the paper, folded it then absent-mindedly tucked it down into her bra.

She glanced up, saw him watching and shook her head.

'Silly habit! I've tucked things in my bra ever since I grew breasts and had to wear one. Problem is I forget I put them there, then later, when I get undressed, the paper tends to stick to the skin so more often than not I step under the shower with it still attached to my person and end up with a very wet and totally unreadable note.'

It was nothing more than an admission of a small folly, yet the image of her stripping off her clothes and stepping naked, except for a folded scrap of napkin, into the shower was so vivid he felt his loins tighten.

'Perhaps you should retrieve it now,' he heard himself say, and knew he wanted to see her delve into that secret place again.

'Or try to improve my memory,' she countered, smiling now so the little lines fanned out at the corner of her eyes and a slight dimple pressed into her right cheek.

Hadn't noticed that before. Had he never been on this side of her when she smiled? Realised she'd asked him something, begged her pardon…

Had to get his wits in order.

'I wondered how your bowel obstruction patient was?' she repeated, and he frowned at her.

'What made you ask that?' he demanded. 'Why would I know?'

The dimple pressed deeper.

'Because you've been up to visit him twice today so I assumed he'd had surgery of some kind. For all your warnings about not getting involved, is it such a bad thing to want to follow through on patients we admit from down here? Is it against protocol?'

He sighed.

'Theoretically, we don't have time to cover all the work down here and keep up with what's happening upstairs as well, but to me it's half the reward, knowing the good stuff that happens after we've dealt with a patient in Emergency. For instance, the latest on Mr Grayson, the heart-attack victim, is that he'll be going home next Tuesday and Albert—the bowel obstruction—had a carcinoma removed but there's no sign of any other trouble so he'll probably be discharged in ten days or so.'

He paused, wanting to ask what had happened to the battered woman—uncertain how to phrase it when he'd just finished telling her it was no concern of hers to follow through with the patient. Social workers were employed for that, but somehow he knew Anna Crane hadn't left the job to them.

'My battered patient—the broken nose—is still living at home. The mother won't budge,' she said, as if she'd read the question in his mind.

'We can't make them move to safety,' he said, sensing a deeper sadness within her and wondering about her past—her early life—pre-husbands. Or had the first incumbent been a batterer? Is that why they'd divorced?

It was frustrating to think how little he knew about her, though why he wanted to know more he couldn't decide. Perhaps so he could carry out the stepchildren's request. Surely knowing more about her, what made her tick, it would help him match her up with someone.

Which reminded him of a few single non-medical mates who were currently unattached—or ready to be unattached. Excused himself and went to phone them. And phone Liz about catering. The sooner Anna Crane was fixed up with a man the better, as far as he was concerned.

CHAPTER THREE

ANNA was good, he'd decided by Friday afternoon. Calm and competent, unflappable in a crisis, easy-mannered with all the patients but firm when she had to be. And the patients sensed it, relating to her, relaxing as she stitched or bound or X-rayed them. In fact the emergency room was running as smoothly as he could remember for a long time.

He was dealing with a teenager's leg wound, a two-inch gash which should have been stitched when the accident occurred but was now red and angry, suppurating—unable to be closed until the infection had been cleared up. He took a culture for Pathology, helped Kim flood it with sterile water and Betadine, and explained to the young man and his mother that it would have to be bathed and cleanly dressed each day.

'Will you be able to manage that at home?' he asked the woman. 'If not, you could bring him into Outpatients.'

'I'll do it,' she said grimly. 'And if it hurts, it will be his own fault. I wanted to bring him in for stitches when it first happened, but he told me I was fussing, and now look at it. He could lose his leg, I told him.'

Pete smiled at the woman's anger, knowing it masked concern.

'I think you've got him here in time to save the leg,' he said, then he turned to the patient. 'But your mother's right. An infection like that could get into the bone, and if that were to happen, losing part of your leg isn't such an unlikely outcome.'

'I know, I know,' the lad grumbled. 'But she does fuss!'

'All mothers do,' a voice said cheerfully, and he turned to see Anna walking into the cubicle, coming close enough to peer at the wound. 'Hmm, nasty!'

'You want something?' he asked, telling himself it was ridiculous to be disturbed by her presence. He was never disturbed by the presence of any of the nurses.

'A second opinion in cubicle four when you've got a moment,' she said quietly, and off she went.

'That's Josh Crane's mum,' the youth said to his mother. 'He said she'd gone back to work. Pity, really. We always spent more at the canteen when she was on duty, she's such a good-looker—great legs and her shape—wow!'

The mother scolded, but the dreamy look in her son's eyes revealed that the message was being ignored. Pete wondered if he'd lusted after older women when at school—hadn't there been a generously endowed English teacher who'd featured in his teenage dreams and fantasies? But that had been different—surely! He handed the dressings to Kim, spoke to the mother.

'Bathe it with Betadine and dress it with sterile dressings every day, then bring him back here in three days and we'll see if it's ready to be stitched.'

He left the room and resisted the temptation to sneak a look at Anna's legs as he walked into cubicle four, although there was enough of them on view as she bent over the patient, intent on some injury to the hand of a bulky, overweight man, a huge man, looming high above the doctor as he sat on the examination table. He had the look that suggested 'bikie', his bald head decorated with red and blue tattoos. Similar decorations crawled up his arms and flowed across his chest, only partly hidden by the black singlet which he'd chosen as his 'going to the hospital' attire in spite of the chilly weather.

'It's a dog bite,' Anna explained to Pete, excusing herself and turning away from the patient. 'The puncture holes are deep but I've X-rayed it and there are no fractures.' She waved a hand towards the film, lit up on the box on the wall. 'I can't see any tendon damage or joint involvement but I'm concerned about infection...'

Infection spread rapidly in tendon sheaths and joint spaces, and could cause permanent damage, with crippling and scarring.

'I'd admit,' he said quietly. 'I know it's a bit extreme but the alternative could be worse. Want me to tell him?'

She grinned at him. 'Think I'm a coward?'

Her smile was still hovering around her lips as she turned back to the man mountain.

'This is Dr Jackson, who's an expert in emergency medicine,' she began. 'He agrees

with me that you should be admitted to hospital—'

'For a dog bite?' the mountain roared. 'It's
a clean dog, my dog. I've been bit before. He
went a little deep, didn't mean it, fooling
around we were. I thought I'd better have a
shot or two, that's all I came here for.'

'I'll give you a tetanus shot and also antibiotics, but we won't really know if you're developing a deep-seated infection unless we
keep an eye on you. If you're here, nurses will
be able to take your temperature regularly,
check the wound, notice any change at all, so
if the dog did leave any nasty bacteria in your
flesh we can put you straight onto stronger antibiotics.'

'My dog don't have nasty bacteria and I
won't stay,' the man stated with uncompro-
mising firmness. 'You give me the shots, wrap
it up and let me out of here.'

Pete waited, unwilling to leave Anna with
so much male aggression but not wanting to
interfere with her treatment of the patient. How
would she tackle it?

'That's OK,' she said easily. 'A lot of people are scared of going into hospital. Can you

remember when you last had a tetanus injection?'

'I ain't scared,' he roared at her. 'It's me dog. Who'll take care of him?'

Anna nodded. 'Yes, that's a problem.' Pete held his breath, ready to stop her if she offered to take on a dog which had already bitten its owner quite severely. 'About the tetanus?'

'Not since school,' the man conceded. 'Eight, maybe ten years ago. Busted me leg coming off me bike and had gravel rash all over me arse. Remember they gave me one then.'

'A tetanus injection, please, Carol.' Anna looked across the table to the nurse who was hovering on the other side of the bed, looking part-fascinated, part-terrified by the man, then she turned back to her patient. 'I'll wrap your hand and put a special dressing on it. It's like a mitten and is supposed to immobilise it so don't go taking it off or fooling around, trying to move your fingers. And you'll keep it in a sling and you'll rest it completely—do you understand?'

She spoke so firmly Pete fully expected the chap to mutter in the exasperated voice he'd used to his own mother when she'd nagged at him, 'Yes, Mum!'

'Yes, ma'am!' the patient said instead—not far out.

Anna seemed satisfied—or was she? She wrapped the hand, slid a mitten over the bandages, wrote out a script for an antibiotic, then held it, apparently not yet ready to pass it over.

'Did you come here on your bike?' she asked.

A nod of the multi-coloured head in reply.

'Well, you can't go home on it. Do you have a mate you'd trust to ride it, and someone else to drive him here?'

The man looked startled, opened his mouth to argue, caught the determination in Anna's eyes and shrugged.

'Will you trust me to make a phone call with me left hand?' he demanded, and she smiled, defusing the last remnants of tension in the small cubicle.

'I reckon I could trust you to do that. Here's your script. Phone your friends then take it to the hospital pharmacy—they'll fix it up for you while you're waiting for your lift. And either go to your local GP or come back here tomorrow—every day for a week, in fact. Once infection sets in it could mean an operation to remove the damaged tissues, and that's nasty.'

The fellow slid to his feet, towering over Anna, and glanced across her head at Pete.

'She serious?' he asked.

'Deadly so, mate,' he replied. 'It's your choice to go home, but you keep it still and have a doctor check it every day. Infection in your hand can end up a real nightmare.'

'I'll come back here,' he promised, patted Anna on the head with his good hand and said cheerfully, 'Thanks, Doc.' Then he lumbered out.

'Phew!' Anna said, waving her hand in front of her face and pretending to collapse back on the table. 'I'm glad you stuck around for that. I had no idea how he was going to react to the possibility of hospitalisation.'

'You handled it well,' Pete assured her, although he hadn't liked the way the man had touched her—even on the head—and wondered if he should have a talk about letting patients become too familiar.

He'd never had such a talk with other team members prior to Anna, and there'd been women among them—junior doctors, usually, pushed into the emergency rooms as part of their training, crossing off the days until they could escape to the upper regions of the hospital.

Would Anna stay? She spoke as if this was what she wanted to do—but, then, if she did remarry—

'I beg your pardon?'

Why did he keep doing this—drifting off into his thoughts and missing her conversation?

He caught her wide, clear eyes fixed on his face and wondered if he looked as divorced from reality as he felt.

'I wondered what time tomorrow night—and is it casual or dressy?'

'Ah, time.' Hell, he must have told the other guests a time—told Liz a time. Eight sounded a bit late. Maybe he'd said—

'Seven, and comfortable as far as dress is concerned.' Listened to the words himself and decided they sounded rational enough. Remembered after she'd followed Wendy into a cubicle with the next patient that he'd told the others seven-thirty. What was happening to him?

Hadn't time to consider it as the next patient arrived, a workman from the local quarry, holding a pad to one eye.

'Did you injure it or get something in it?' he asked, as he ushered the man into a cubicle.

'Something in it—dust or dirt. Wind's blowing something fierce out there.'

'Let's take a look,' Pete suggested, asking him to sit in the adjustable chair he could tilt back to get a clear view of the injured eye. 'I'll put in a drop of anaesthetic,' he explained, as Kim brought in an eye tray and set it on the trolley. 'That will make it feel better while I examine it.'

There was nothing to be seen, which didn't surprise him. Most eye pain was caused either by a disease, like herpes simplex, or, with sudden onset, by a foreign body causing corneal abrasion, which continued to hurt long after lachrymal fluid had washed the intruder away.

'Does it feel better?' he asked.

'Yes, you bet,' the man replied so Pete knew he could proceed with an investigation.

'I'll use a dye to see if I can pinpoint the problem,' he told his patient, dropping in fluorescein dye and moving a slit lamp closer to take a look.

Three small scratches appeared, bright greeny-yellow in colour and fixed in position.

'It's an abrasion,' he explained, 'and will be painful for a few days. I'll anaesthetise it again, but that will only last perhaps fifteen minutes. It will begin to hurt again and you'll feel as if there's half a brick in it for about twenty-four hours. I can help it a bit with another type of drop and I'll use some antibiotic cream to prevent infection, but I'd like you to come back here or go to your own doctor tomorrow. If it's not improving, you may have to be referred to a specialist.'

The man seemed unperturbed, standing up and patting the patch Wendy had fitted over it.

'Few days off on compo might be just what a bloke needs,' he said, then he frowned. 'Damn it all, tomorrow's Saturday. I'll probably be as good as new by Monday. You here on Saturdays?'

Pete shook his head.

'Not this Saturday,' he said, thinking of the work he'd have to do, tidying his house before guests arrived. 'We work different rotations every three months and I've not long come off nights and weekends. Paul Wells will be the man on duty tomorrow. Pop in and see him.'

He saw the patient out, thinking of the party—if dinner for eight people could be called a party. Liz had agreed to act as hostess as well as organise the food, claiming it was a good advertisement for the new catering service she was offering.

Wondered what Liz would think of Anna—

'Ambulance on the way,' Margie called. 'Which of you lucky people wants a school playground accident?'

'I'll take it, I've had lunch and Pete's just come out of a cubicle,' he heard Anna say, and swung around to see her right behind him, smiling.

'Not only organising *my* department but creeping up on me now?' he growled, hiding the strange quiver in his belly which her smile was starting to generate.

'Off you go,' she said, ignoring his rebuke and walking towards the electronically operated doors. 'That's the ambulance arriving now. I'll yell for you if I need help.'

He went, reluctantly—not because he didn't need some sustenance but because he was getting used to having her around. He quite liked working with her on a patient, or having her work with him.

She didn't yell and, with no patients needing attention, he ate an uninterrupted lunch then settled in his office to attack the stack of paperwork which found its way on to his desk with the persistence and dedication of ants at a picnic.

He had a department heads meeting at three-thirty and, for once, his department had remained quiet, although voices inside a cubicle told him Anna had another patient.

Telling Margie where to find him if she needed him, he took off—how to get more money for the department from the hospital budget in the forefront of his mind.

'Has Dr Crane left?' he asked Kelly Dunne, the receptionist on the evening shift, when he eventually returned—the department no richer and his temper simmering with frustration.

Kelly stared at him as if she didn't know who Dr Crane was, shrugged, tossed her head and said in a snippy voice, 'How would I know?'

'Because I assume she'd say goodbye,' he retorted. 'You've been on duty since four—did you see her go?'

Another head-toss business, dark silky waves of hair slapping around her shoulders. 'I didn't see her,' she snorted, and glared at him.

This was ridiculous. He and Kelly had shared some laughs together down at the local, gone out for a meal a couple of times, seen a movie together. What was biting her?

Ask, his sisters always said. Open lines of communication!

He asked.

'Why are you so snippy?'

Saw her eyes narrow, her lips move as if she was repeating his adjective, the hair fling itself about again.

'Snippy?' The word was repeated aloud this time. 'That's good! I thought we were friends,

Pete Jackson, then next thing I hear you're throwing a party for half the hospital and I'm not invited. Wouldn't that make you feel...' She paused and he knew what was coming. 'Snippy?'

He felt his eyes roll back in his head. Women!

'I am not throwing a party, nor is half the hospital coming,' he said coolly—after all, what business was it of hers whom he invited to his house? That was the trouble with even the most casual of relationships with the opposite sex. They got things all wrong.

Tried a half-truth. 'In fact, only six people are coming, most of them new staff. My cousin Liz has started a catering business and I thought I'd help her advertise it among these newcomers to town.'

'Dr Crane isn't a newcomer to town. She's lived here for years.'

Closed his eyes this time, counted to ten—twelve and a half. Decided he didn't really need to appease Kelly—remembered he'd decided he didn't want to take their tentative friendship any further after the last time they'd met at the pub.

On the other hand, he didn't want to upset her. The staff in Emergency were a tight-knit group. Wondered how the truth would sound.

'She's new on the staff and I thought, as she's currently single and the new chap in O and G, Ken, is also single, they might match up together.'

Kelly shrieked with laughter, which was better than the head-tossing routine but the noise made the few people still waiting in Outpatients all turn towards them.

'You a matchmaker? Now I've heard everything. The man who runs a mile if a woman even begins to get serious actually setting up some other poor patsy! Really, Pete, that's too much.'

She turned to greet a patient, still chuckling, and he left the building puzzling over what she'd said. Was that his reputation in the hospital? And did he run a mile whenever a relationship began to develop?

He supposed he had with Kelly—well, not run a mile, but begun avoiding places they'd both frequented.

But he'd known it had no future and liked her too much to get involved then hurt her.

Wasn't that reasonable? Wouldn't any man do the same?

Began to doubt himself, to wonder.

He unlocked his car, climbed in, tilted the rear-view mirror and studied himself as he'd seen women do.

Did he know himself at all? Know the chap with the craggy features, dark hair and strange greenish eyes who stared back at him? Did he have any idea what made him tick?

He flipped the mirror back into position. Of course he did—he knew himself really well. There was no need for this doubt and self-analysis.

Yet the questions lingered in his head—not taking precedence, cleaning the house was doing that—like the low notes in a musical composition. So when his brother phoned—Callum, the oldest of the three boys in the family—he asked him about the running-a-mile business, growling angrily when Callum answered with another question, 'Who knows you that well?'

'I've had plenty of very happy and satisfying relationships,' he protested.

'Ten years ago—maybe even seven. When was Kate?'

'Kate didn't want to marry me any more than I wanted to marry her,' he argued. 'And there've been women in my life since then.'

'Too many, according to our mother,' Callum replied, 'and too few according to our sisters. But that isn't why I phoned. I heard Anna Crane had gone back to work in an emergency department. I know she was living in Huntley. Is she with you?'

'How the hell do you know Anna Crane?' Pete demanded, feeling as if his world was spinning off its axle.

Callum laughed.

'Ted Crane was a specialist here at the Royal until he got too sick to work. He'd kind of been a mentor to Anna—since she was at school apparently. She always said she'd become a doctor because of Ted. Anyway, when he learned he had perhaps twelve months to live Anna took over, giving up her job and marrying him to give the kids some security, some continuity in their lives. Their mother had been killed in a car accident when they were toddlers and Ted had brought them up.

'I just wanted to ask you to keep an eye on her, help her ease back into work. She's special, that woman—she deserves the best.'

Pete heard his brother's words and made some appropriate reply, which must have been acceptable for Callum said goodbye and hung up on him—but his main trouble was collating the information. What was it that had brought Anna Crane's life into collision with his, and what did she have that such disparate people as his brother and her stepchildren were concerned about her well-being?

He gave up on the housework, phoning a woman who 'did' for him when he was desperate and begging her to come in the following morning. Sat down and brooded after the woman agreed, replaying the few non-medical conversations he'd had with Dr Crane. Recalled the ripple effect of the red curls, their contrast with her pale skin where they touched her shoulders, wondered what she'd wear that was 'comfortable'—sorry he hadn't said formal—picturing her in something black and slinky which would reveal even more bare, pale skin…

The vision was so vivid he stood up and hit his head with his hand, certain he was losing his mind. Answered the phone, wondering if it was someone else soliciting aid for Anna, and heard her voice filter along the wires like a ghost tapping him unexpectedly on the shoulder.

'I know you're off duty and probably have social arrangements for the evening but could you possibly come back to the hospital?'

'I'm on my way,' he answered, not bothering to ask why. Her tone had held the strain of desperation, as if she was holding on by a very fine margin to her customary control.

She was in one of the emergency trauma rooms and had obviously been there for some time, which explained why she hadn't said goodbye. Her patient was a woman who would still be classed as middle-aged if life had treated her more kindly. He glanced at the battered face, the dried, caked blood on the swollen lips, and wondered if Anna was unlucky in attracting victims of domestic violence or if this was the mother. A nurse he didn't know was standing slightly behind Anna, and the tension in the room was taut enough to feel—like electric currents on a windy day.

'Is there a problem, Dr Crane?' he demanded in his most officious voice.

She looked up from the drip she was adjusting in the patient's arm and he saw relief flood cross her expressive face—hoped like hell he wasn't about to disappoint her.

'I want to admit Mrs Jennings,' she said quietly. 'She was brought in by ambulance—a neighbour called it for her. She has a severe head wound, is comatose, pupils unevenly dilated. We're running fluids into her but can't stabilise her blood pressure so I believe there's internal bleeding somewhere.'

She glanced towards the corner of the room where a man stood glowering at her.

'Mr Jennings wants to take her home.'

She should have called the police, not me. That was his first thought, then he saw the plea in her eyes, felt her trying to tell him something he had to know, to remind him of something.

The daughter?

She'd refused to leave the abusive environment because he'd beat the mother if she did—but if the mother was removed, who was left?

'Admit the patient. I'll take care of Mr Jennings,' he said quietly. He looked towards the miserable worm who had to make something of himself by lashing out at the women in his household and added, 'Then expedite a transfer of the other patient to Crystal Creek as soon as possible, Dr Crane. If you'd come this way, Mr Jennings, I'll explain the procedures.'

'I don't have to come with you and you can't admit her without consent. I know the rules,' the man declared, backing into a corner of the room.

'I can admit any badly injured patient as an emergency—even operate without consent if I wish,' Pete said, hoping he looked as haughty and authoritative as he'd tried to sound. He took the man's arm, steering him towards the office, determined to tell him a few home truths.

But nothing was ever that easy. The man spun around, grabbing at the fluid bag and reefing it from the drip stand, splattering the clear liquid in all directions as the tube came free. Anna reacted instinctively, bending over her patient, detaching the tube with swift, sure fingers before it, too, was reefed out of the vein.

Orderlies, alerted by the nurse, arrived, two strong young men who grabbed the struggling, swearing man and propelled him from the room.

'Where do you want him, Doc?'

'In my office, and I'd like you both to stay if you could. I'll need witnesses to this conversation.' And possibly protection if he decides to take a swing at me.

As he followed them towards his office, he signalled to Kelly to phone the police. It was a sign all the staff knew and understood, but one they were reluctant to use. Police intervention often exacerbated domestic situations so they tried to sort things out themselves whenever possible.

But not this time. If hc had any say in the matter, neither Miss nor Mrs Jennings would ever see the man again. And if he could have him arrested and detained overnight, it would give them breathing space to move Miss Jennings from the house—even allow her to pack clothes and personal items for herself and her mother.

'I know I should have handled that myself,' Anna apologised later, when the police had taken Mr Jennings to the watch house and all the formalities of his arrest and his wife's admittance had been finalised.

'I'll do better in future, but I was so worried about the daughter and didn't know if the police would act on our complaint and actually keep him out of the way while I organised her. I've phoned Crystal Creek and they'll have her, but with her mother in hospital I don't think she'll go because transport's so difficult from out there. Does the hospital have a flat or rooms where she could stay for a few days?'

He nodded his agreement, then shook his head as exasperation with her grew.

'I'll go along with you on this because it's a special case, but you shouldn't get too involved with your patients—do you remember that rule?'

She grinned at him, her eyes sparkling, crinkling at the corners—like sapphires, not the sky at all.

'I'll try to,' she promised, 'but about the room?'

'Persistent piece, aren't you?' He sighed. 'Yes, there's accommodation here. The Red Cross run that particular service. I'll speak to someone about it. You'll have to find her—if a neighbour called the ambulance, you'd think the same person would have told Miss Jennings what's happened.'

'She works quite late—in a fish and chip shop. She's probably not home yet. The father also holds down a regular job which is why she can leave her mother during the day—then he goes to the pub after work and Janice usually arrives home before him. For some reason, he must have gone home early today and taken out his temper on his wife.'

'He was sacked,' Pete told her, explaining that the police had got that much information out of him. 'Left the job at twelve, had a few beers, then went home and bashed his wife because someone else had upset him.'

He saw the shudder ripple through her body, and touched her gently on the shoulder.

'I'm glad you called me,' he said. 'Now, isn't it time you were getting home to those kids of yours?'

'Oh, I've rung them to say I'll be late. I'll go out to the Jennings house and speak to Janice, bring her back here, then head home.'

'I can get someone from the social work department to do that,' he protested. 'They always have staff on call.'

His protest fell on deaf ears. She smiled again and shook her head so the curls bounced and jostled with each other.

'She knows me. I'll go.'

'Then I'll come with you,' he announced. 'In fact, we'll take my car. I think she should get all their personal stuff out of the house while we know he's locked up. If he's off work, who knows when she might be able to get back in there again? I've got a big Land Cruiser—it will hold more.'

His 'team' looked surprised, then amused.

'And you were telling me not to get involved? You're way ahead of me in the involvement stakes here!'

'Been there before,' he said grimly. 'Only that time it was a woman with three small children and we didn't get them out in time. I go with instincts now—and yours seem good enough for both of us to follow in this case.'

She touched him gently on the arm—a 'there, there,' kind of pat—and he wondered if the regret he still felt over the Fuller case had been so evident in his voice.

CHAPTER FOUR

NOT one of his better ideas. The Land Cruiser wasn't nearly as big as Pete had thought it— the space limitation bringing his passenger uncomfortably close for the drive to the Jennings' house. He opened the windows to see if that would help—at least remove the elusive fragrance which hung about her like a cloud of flowers.

But, no, the stream of air simply stirred it up, making him more, not less, aware of her.

'It's the next street on the left,' she said, apparently as oblivious to his body as he was alert to every movement of hers. 'Then the fourth house down. There are lights on.'

Janice Jennings was in the front yard, another woman with her, and even in the dim glow of the streetlight Pete saw her cringe as the car pulled up.

Anna must have seen it too. 'I'll get out first,' she said quickly, unbuckling her seat belt and opening the door as he pulled into the kerb. 'Hi, Janice—it's me, Anna Crane from the hospital.'

Pete saw the woman sway, then sink to the ground. Fainted! They were doing fine so far. Poor blighter probably thought her mother was dead. He scrambled out and hurried to where Anna had raised Janice to a sitting position and was speaking low and urgently. He introduced himself to the stranger—the neighbour who'd phoned for an ambulance.

'She came racing out of the house with him after her, but she's weak—can barely walk most of the time—so she tripped and fell right here on the lawn and I knew I had to do something. The police—they hate coming to domestics so I phoned the ambulance then told him both it and the police were on the way and he vamoosed.'

'Well, he ended up at the hospital and we had him arrested there,' Pete told her. 'They'll only be able to hold him until he appears before a magistrate in the morning, and even with a restraining order against him I think he'll probably come after his daughter.'

'Course he would,' the neighbour agreed. 'Those orders aren't worth the paper they're written on. My daughter...'

Pete tuned out and bent down to help Janice to her feet. He listened as Anna spoke persuasively, telling her this was her chance to get away.

'But it's my house,' Janice protested. 'I worked for the money for it, bought it myself. I hate to think he'll end up here while we're hiding away in some shelter.'

'He'll be jailed eventually for the attack on your mother. If you stay somewhere else until his trial comes up, then you can reclaim the house, maybe sell it and move to a new address.'

'If Mum agrees,' she said doubtfully, and Anna patted her arm.

'One thing at a time,' she said, although Pete was sure, from the concern on her face, that she doubted Mrs Jennings would be making decisions for a long time to come. 'Let's gather up some things for both you and your mother, and get you over to the hospital. Your mother's unconscious now, but I'm sure you'll want to be near her when she wakes. What about your job? Should I call someone and let them know you won't be in for a while?'

Tactful soul, this Anna Crane, Pete thought. She hasn't told Janice to stay away from places where her father might look for her, but she'd given the woman the idea so she could work it out for herself.

'If you would,' Janice replied, apparently content to put her future in Anna's hands after that initial protest.

He stood about like an unneeded spare part until Anna called to him from a bedroom.

'There are these two cases—that's all Janice wants to take,' she said, pointing to the battered old suitcases sitting on the floor of a small bedroom. 'She's just packing some stuff for her mother.'

He lifted the two suitcases, then set them down, realising Anna was both looking and sounding worried about something. In fact, she looked so pale he wondered how she was standing upright, and there was an air of fragility about her robust frame. Made him want to put his arm around her—give her a hug.

Daft thought!

'What's the problem?'

She glanced at him, and offered a weak smile.

'I really hate this kind of thing,' she muttered. 'I can't help wondering if I'm interfering for the good of the patient or because I think it's right for her—or them in this case.'

There was more than that behind her sudden decline but he understood where she was coming from with her hesitation—the second thoughts.

'Go with instinct,' he advised, 'and in this particular case, I think your instincts are sound.'

The urge to hug her—offer physical comfort—returned so he picked up the suitcases and headed for the car before he got himself into strife.

She chatted to Janice all the way to the hospital, where she handed her over to a Red Cross volunteer, promising to call in and see her mother some time the following day. Then, as the two departed, the suitcases stacked on a purloined gurney, she sighed.

'Tired?' he asked. 'Would you like me to drive you home? It would be no bother—I could even collect you in the morning and bring you back to get your car.'

He couldn't believe it was his mouth saying such things—didn't know if he wanted her to say yes or no.

Guessed she was equally confused as she hesitated.

'No, that's far too much bother for you,' she protested—after too long a pause. Then she held out her hands and he saw the tremble in them. 'Actually, if you don't mind driving me home, I can get Josh to drive me back tomorrow. He's recently passed his test and loves any excuse to show off his prowess.'

He waited while she fetched her briefcase from the office, then led her back out to the car. Saw her glance at her watch, frown, then shrug. Waited, because he was beginning to know this was one woman who thought through what she said before she let the words escape.

'The kids are ordering pizza. It might be a bit limp and tired by the time we get there—I'd told them eight o'clock—but you'd be welcome to stay and eat with us if you like.'

Definitely not, his head said, but once again his mouth seemed to be doing its own thing—he could have sworn he heard himself say how much he enjoyed warmed-up pizza, and if that wasn't a yes, he didn't know what was.

The house was a sprawling wooden building with wide, sheltered verandahs around four sides and a magnificent view out over the lights of the large country town from the back one. It was obvious this was where the family spent most of their time—comfortable canvas chairs, plenty of small tables to hold books, papers, drinks or snacks, and a round table where the two teenagers were arguing amiably over their pizza.

'Dr Jackson, hi!'

Josh rose to his feet as he greeted him, holding out his hand. Jackie was less assertive—a smile of welcome and a shy hello.

'It's been a long day so Dr Jackson drove me home,' Anna explained, and Pete saw Josh bristle slightly.

'I'd have picked you up if you'd phoned me,' he grumbled. He subsided as Anna ruffled her hand in his dreadful hair and said, 'I know you would, but he was handier. Anyway, it means I've left my car in the parking lot so you can drive me back tomorrow.'

Broad smile as if all was made right again.

'Would you like a cold drink?' Josh offered. 'There's some light beer in the refrigerator. I don't drink but Anna usually has a glass of wine with her dinner and she always keeps some beer in case visitors pop in.'

Beer-drinking visitors? Why am I looking for someone for the woman if she already has male visitors?

Missed her conversation again. Something about bathrooms. Said no to a beer—even light. He was having enough trouble controlling his senses while stone cold sober.

'It's this way,' Jackie said, as Anna disappeared into the house. Obviously the girl had been deputed to show him where to wash his hands. His mother's reminder of this task rang in his head, wondered what she'd think of Anna, more or less telling him the same thing.

He followed Jackie through the huge living area inside, across polished wooden floors with large carpets defining dining and sitting areas, along a wide passage to a room on the right. It was a bathroom as big as most bedrooms in modern houses, small black and white tiles making a checkered pattern on the floor, the old bath-tub, long enough for a man as tall as he was to stretch out in—claw-footed—enamelled black outside.

Great room! Great house. Thought of the town-house he'd recently acquired—a sensible size for a man who intended staying single—clean, new, practical. Who in their right mind would want a rambling old place like this? Washed his hands and dried them, wondering why the house appealed to him—knowing he couldn't be in his right mind to even be thinking this way.

But the mood persisted—perhaps because of the relaxed interaction with the Crane children, their gentle teasing of their stepmother, their respectful but not shy or bashful behaviour towards him.

'This was our grandfather's house,' Josh told him. 'Our dad's father. He died the year before Dad got sick, but before we lived here we always came for holidays so when Dad suggested coming back to Huntley, Jackie and Anna and I all thought it was a great idea. Our great-grandfather built the place—milled the timber from cypress pines which grew on his property up in the hills. He needed so much he bought the mill, but it was shut down a long time ago. After great-grandfather died.'

Pete listened to them talk of the past—of death—and marvelled that youngsters who'd seen so much of it at close quarters should be so well adjusted. Wondered how much Anna's quiet presence had to do with it. She hadn't contributed much during the evening and he sensed she was still concerned over the Jennings family, but both Jackie and Josh turned to her frequently—for confirmation or approval—checking dates, bits of family history, as if they knew she knew their family legends, was a real part of them.

'I'd better be off,' he said, when the pizza boxes had been removed, coffee enjoyed and the conversation flagging as first Jackie, then Josh excused themselves to go to bed.

'Thanks for bringing me home,' Anna said, standing up with such alacrity he wondered if she'd been waiting for him to make a move. 'I'll walk you out.'

'Afraid I'll get lost?' he asked, annoyed with her—and himself—and not knowing why.

'Being polite,' she retorted crisply, picking up on his mood and turning it back on him. 'But the thanks are heartfelt—not politeness,' she added, a contrite smile chasing around her lips. 'I was too hyped-up to drive. I feel much better now with food and a little conversation.'

He wanted to ask if the children were always as forthcoming about the past, as open about their father's death—a hundred other things which had come up in their talk—but he sensed this wasn't the time so he followed her around the verandah, said goodnight and walked away.

Not looking back although he knew she was there, leaning against the railing, watching until he drove away. Perhaps for longer.

He realised he had absolutely no idea of what was going on inside her head—what she thought of him, either as a colleague or an acquaintance. She wasn't interested in him—he could usually pick up those vibes quite quickly—but, then, why would she be when he'd told her he wasn't available?

So it didn't matter!

But was she interested in any other man?

Asked himself the same question the following evening as he watched her talk and joke and laugh with Ken Riddell and Bill Finch, an engineer he'd known in his student days. Even his mate—a very married mate, David Johnson—seemed taken with her although Pete had seated him beside Liz and few men failed to be impressed by Liz's blonde beauty. He hoped Sally Johnson didn't mind David's interest—she and David had been students with him, and he'd hate to be the cause of trouble between them.

She'd arrived late—Anna—and had apologised profusely when he'd met her at the door. Held up at the hospital, she'd explained, where Mrs Jennings was still in Intensive Care. Janice had phoned her, upset because her father, released on bail, was heading for the hospital to stir up trouble. The neighbour had contacted Janice to let her know.

'Did someone sort him out?' Pete had demanded, annoyed to think Anna might have run into the man who'd see her as the cause of all his problems.

She'd smiled at him.

'My bikie did,' she'd admitted. 'He happened to be in Emergency when the man came blustering in and all he had to do was stand up and tell him to shove off, that he wasn't wanted there. Seems someone had persuaded Janice to go down and get her nose splinted again and she'd met up with Tim—that's the bikie's name—and had been talking to him while she waited.'

'An unlikely pairing,' he'd said, then Liz had called him to say the dinner was ready and he'd introduced Anna around and had sat back to watch the interaction.

Not that he'd minded at first. When he sat back it meant he could study her more closely. She'd pulled all the rioting curls into a plastic clip of some kind on the top of her head, but some were creeping out and trailing down against her temples and at the back of her neck. Nice neck, slender, tilting her head forward as she listened to Ken speak, putting her profile on view to Pete—the straight, elegant nose, fan of laugh-lines by her eyes, dimple dancing as she chuckled at some remark.

Yes, she deserved to find some happiness, he decided, and turned his scrutiny to Ken.

The chap seemed pleasant enough. Linda, the new radiographer he'd invited to even the numbers, certainly seemed to think so. She was flashing smiles at him as well.

'I think it's going well,' Liz whispered to him. 'Everyone seems to be getting on with each other.'

'That's because the food's excellent.'

Liz gave him a quick hug and a grateful kiss on the cheek. 'The wine helped, too,' she reminded him. 'In fact, I think Anna might have to drive everyone home—she's the only one not indulging.'

'Hey, I've only had one glass.' David caught the end of the conversation and argued. 'It's Sally's turn to have a drink so I'm staying sober.' Then he turned to Pete and began to talk about Friday's meeting—as head of the Outpatient Department, he often joined forces with Pete to argue a joint case for more funding.

Sally teased them about talking shop but as she was a surgeon in the department currently receiving the largest hand-outs they hushed her and continued to plot.

Which is why he missed most of the argument which had arisen at the other end of the table. Something to do with the importance of professions—how doctors wouldn't be able to perform half the procedures they did these days if engineers hadn't designed such precise tools. He stayed out of it, enjoying the flush of colour on Anna's cheeks as she threw herself into the fray.

It took them through to midnight, when the Johnsons pleaded a Cinderella babysitter, excused themselves and stood up to go. It signalled a general exodus. Linda asked them for a lift as she lived in that direction, and Anna offered to drive anyone home as she hadn't been drinking, Bill and Ken both accepting with far too much alacrity.

'You could stay the night and drive home in the morning,' Pete suggested to Bill, not wanting his mate to muck up the opportunity for Ken and Anna to be alone. Not that he was so certain about Ken any more. The man seemed to have had too much to drink.

'Ken could come with us,' Sally suggested, turning to the new man with a smile. 'Didn't you say you had a place out Redbridge way?'

Somehow they sorted themselves into cars, Ken going off with Sally, David and Linda, Bill taking Anna's arm in a proprietary way.

'Thank you so much—it was a splendid meal,' Anna said to Liz, who surprised Pete by kissing his guest on the cheek.

'And thank you so much for thinking of it,' she added to Pete, holding out her hand to shake his. 'It was the best night I've had for ages.'

'We must do it again,' he heard himself blathering, while he watched Bill edging closer to the woman he barely knew and putting a guiding hand beneath her elbow. Wondered why he'd asked him. He'd always been too much of a ladies' man—that Bill!

'Most successful—they were all fun people,' Liz declared. 'Now you can help me clear away the mess and tell me why I haven't heard any hints about this Anna from someone in the family.'

He stared at her, trying to work out what she meant—caught on, and scowled.

'You haven't heard anything because I've only just met her myself. She's a colleague, nothing more. In fact, she once worked with

Callum and he asked me to keep an eye on her.'

'Oh, yes,' Liz said in that infuriating way women had which meant they'd heard you but didn't believe a word you'd said. 'And that Bill's something else!' she continued blithely. 'If I didn't have my Jason coming back to town any day, I'd have had a flirt with him myself. A very sexy and attractive man.'

Bill sexy and attractive?

Perhaps he was—he always seemed to have some woman in tow.

But was he reliable? Anna was the marrying kind. Wasn't Bill one of those men whom Josh had characterised as only wanting one thing from a woman?

'I shouldn't have let Anna drive him home,' he muttered, the words 'sexy and attractive' hammering in his head. They conjured up images of Bill making a move—his hand on her bare shoulder—the pale skin—

'Relax,' Liz told him. 'I'm certain Anna can take care of herself for all Callum asking you to keep an eye on her. She's a very sensible lady and I doubt she'd be taken in by Bill's charm.'

'But that's what I'm trying to do,' he protested, contrarily upset now that his grand plan
might not work. 'Only I did think Ken would
suit, not Bill.'

'And you invited Linda for yourself, I'd
guess.' She patted his arm the way his sisters
did when they thought they knew more than
he did. 'Don't worry. Ken's interested in Anna
as well so I think you'll find Linda's free for
you. Want to bet double or quits my fee that
Ken'll be phoning Anna tomorrow?'

'No, I don't want to bet,' he said, sounding
just as snippy as Kelly had the day before.
'And this conversation is ridiculous. Since
you're staying the night, why don't you go to
bed? I'll clean up the kitchen.'

She needed no persuading, kissed him on
the cheek and disappeared upstairs, heading
for the bedroom where she'd left her overnight
things.

'Was Bill going to share my bedroom or
yours,' she called back down to him, 'when
you offered to have him stay over?'

He ignored the jibe, knowing she'd guessed
he'd made the offer because he didn't want
Anna driving the other man home.

She was right, of course, but if she knew why he'd felt that way then she knew more than he did.

By Monday morning Pete had decided that he'd done all he need do as far as his new colleague was concerned. He'd satisfied the Crane children's request to introduce her to a couple of eligible men, and as for Callum's plea to keep an eye on her, well, he could do that at work—on a strictly professional basis, of course.

And it worked well right through Monday, though why an O and G specialist should choose to have lunch in the emergency department lounge he didn't know.

Or didn't want to know.

'We should sit down and review last week's case notes,' he said to Anna, interrupting what was too like a tête-à-tête for him to be comfortable about joining. 'I'll be in my office when you've finished lunch.'

She came within minutes, unruffled by his abrupt demand, pulling a chair over to his desk so she could read the files he had piled on its surface.

'Is there anything I'm doing wrong?' she asked first, looking at him with anxious eyes and making him feel a heel.

'Of course not,' he assured her. 'Well, you could have called the police when Mr Jennings became abusive but we've already discussed that and it's a very fine line. Tim Fisher's hand is obviously healing well—probably well enough to discontinue visits so there's no need to hand his file over to Outpatients.'

Felt a movement from the other chair, sensed she was wondering whether to speak or keep her mouth shut. He went on, explaining how patients could return to the emergency room for dressings over the weekend when Outpatients was closed, but files were passed on after that.

She wasn't with him—he knew that—still considering whatever was tucked away in her convoluted female mind.

'Out with it,' he commanded, and saw a wash of pink sweep up her cheeks like a strawberry milkshake spreading beneath her skin.

'Well, he's been such a help,' she began, her voice unusually tentative for a woman of such firm opinions, 'with Janice Jennings.'

Her eyes met his, pleading for his under-standing. 'I know they seem the most unlikely couple but I think—I'm almost sure—they might be falling in love.'

He choked on his surprise, shook his head and glared at her.

'I hope David Johnson doesn't realise you'll be using his outpatient department as a lonely hearts' club,' he told her. 'If there's no need to continue treatment he shouldn't be coming in.'

She nodded, totally unabashed as far as he could see.

'I'll have a talk to him,' she said. 'Actually, it's probably better if he hangs around in the ICU waiting room. That's where Jennings is more likely to turn up.'

Pete straightened in his chair, deciding it was time he took control of this situation. 'We can't have people acting as vigilantes in this hospital. We have Security for characters like Jennings.'

'But they're not always around when you actually need them,' she pointed out with ir-refutable logic. 'And he won't vigilante—if it's a verb. All he has to do is stand up.

According to the staff who were on duty on Saturday, Mr Jennings took one look at him and fled. That man's a total coward, only capable of tackling weaker people.'

He gave up trying to persuade her that the principle was still faulty and her encouragement of Tim Fisher even more foolhardy. Moved on to the next case, the child with the broken forearm.

'Most of the patients we see but don't admit will go to their local GP for a follow-up consultation. The GP's name is always on the file and we send them a letter with details of the injury or illness and the treatment we've provided, preferably on the same day we see the patient.'

He flicked through the file and saw the copy of the letter to the child's GP. Turned to her, hoping he didn't appear as surprised as he felt.

'When did you do this? You were flat out Friday afternoon, and then attending to Mrs Jennings until well into the evening.'

She grinned at him as if pleased by his surprise.

'I popped in and did some paperwork on Saturday when Josh dropped me off to collect my car. And don't tell me you don't do the same. The receptionist on duty told me you'd just left.'

He scowled at her, not pleased at all.

'You'll burn out if you don't pace yourself,' he muttered, moving on to the next file, explaining how less urgent letters were sent out to the GPs of patients who were admitted.

'We've clerical staff who can handle the typing but with computerised filing I find it easier to do my own than to write a note to the typist, telling her what I want to say.'

Anna nodded, and he knew she'd typed the letter he'd seen herself. Which was commendable—so why did he feel annoyed? Because he hadn't caught her out?

No.

Because he was still grouchy over Ken Riddell eating lunch down here?

Surely not.

The woman was a colleague, nothing more. He barely knew her!

'With patients who come back for treatment, usually because they don't have a regular GP, we officially pass the files to Outpatients, but we have access to them when they return for some other reason. The receptionist will get someone to pull old files for you if you need them, say, for a patient who was in a year ago.'

Mind back on track, on work—or so he imagined—until she shifted in her chair—not much, but enough to move the air between them so he caught a faint whiff of perfume and lost his train of thought completely.

Work thought, that is.

'Did you get on OK with Bill—driving him home?' he asked, his mouth out of control once again. 'No trouble with him? No hassles?'

She stared at him, her eyes wide with surprise.

'Should there have been?' she demanded, steel in her voice. 'Did you knowingly allow me to drive the local rapist home? Or what other kind of hassles might I have had?'

Blast the woman—taking umbrage like that.

'I was simply asking,' he said stiffly, hoping she'd realise he was affronted by her attack. 'And there's nothing wrong with Bill but he'd had a few drinks. I wouldn't like to think he'd have, well...' Hell, how did he get out of this one? 'Well, taken advantage of you in any way. Attractive woman and all that...

She chuckled then, umbrage forgotten—which made him angrier.

'He wasn't any trouble,' she assured him, still smiling—almost as if she was amused by the memory of their drive. 'None at all,' she added, and gazed dreamily into space.

Definitely remembering the drive. The swine had obviously kissed her—that's what the soft chuckle and the dazed look in her eyes signified. She'd probably kissed him back—and it hadn't even been a date!

'Excuse me?'

But she'd gone, leaving him vaguely aware that a nurse had come in—and he hadn't heard the call to duty.

Although Anna had.

He walked out to see what was happening. Found Kim, who explained Anna was with a vomiting child in cubicle one and an overdose was about to pull into the ambulance bay—all his!

He put his head around the curtain of cubicle one and saw Anna inserting a drip into the child's arm. She was talking quietly, not to the listless boy but to his mother who was so tense Pete could see the tendons standing out in her neck.

'See if you can persuade the mother to sit down—perhaps have a cup of tea or coffee,' he murmured to Kim, then heard Anna suggest the same thing to Wendy, who was assisting her.

She added, 'He'll be fine, Mrs Roberts, but we'll have to admit him so we don't want you cracking up on us. Wendy will get you a chair to start off with, and as soon as I've got him comfortable we'll transfer him up to the ward.'

He headed for the ambulance bay, well satisfied with his new assistant, knowing she thought like he did about the things that mattered—like patient care, concern for relatives, involvement with the people who came in injured or hurting. In some emergency departments the hype was all—the rush and bustle promoting an atmosphere that said, We deal with injuries not people. He hated conveying that impression, had fought against it, insisting the department have sufficient staff to eliminate the craziness at all but the most frenetic of times.

Which still happened every now and then, although most emergency work was nuts and bolts stuff—accidents from minor to major, illness from vomiting to chest pains. There were sudden, unexpected occurrences which threw both the patient and their immediate supporters into panic. All the folk who came through the door needed an atmosphere of calm control, not more hype and excitement.

Yes, he decided as the ambulance pulled in and the doors were flung open by the waiting staff, Anna Crane was well suited to his kind of emergency care.

But was she as well suited to Bill?

Or Ken Riddell?

CHAPTER FIVE

PETE met the ambulance, surprised to see his 'overdose' patient alert and chatting to the drivers. Then recognised the patient, remembered his history of depression and knew the battle was about to begin. He dragged up facts and figures from the back of his mind—tricyclic antidepressants—TCAs. In something like a quarter of fatal overdose cases the patients had arrived at the emergency treatment centre in a conscious state and with no signs of the usual tachycardia, seizures or coma.

They'd also deteriorated rapidly, he reminded himself, taking the pill bottle from the ambulance bearer and walking beside the gurney into the closest trauma room. Read the label—Tofranil—the prescription date the previous day—not enough prescribed in this bottle to do harm but who could stop a patient hoarding them?

Lester, the lad's name was. Kim had his chart out already and was talking to him—asking when he'd taken them.

'Hook him up for an ECG, then do his vitals while I get a tube into him and clean out his stomach.'

'Do you always use a tube, not ipecac?' Anna had joined them, Wendy following her. 'You want an IV line established?'

He nodded to the second question.

'Get some blood for Pathology first,' he reminded her, then watched her move calmly into action. Wendy passed him a tube and he measured the length against Lester's chest, knowing the young man was enjoying the drama but unable to believe anyone would willingly put their body through this procedure. He explained his actions to Anna, answering the question she'd asked earlier.

'Although he's still awake, I use the tube in case he deteriorates and loses his gag reflex before the ipecac makes him vomit. It also means I can get a slurry of charcoal into his stomach fast—before I wash it out. It might prevent some of the drug being absorbed.'

He poured charcoal down the tube, counted to thirty and applied suction, dragging the assorted mess back out of the patient's stomach, disconnected the suction and used warmed sterile water as a wash, suction again, disconnect, more activated charcoal, mixed this time with a cathartic to help the remnants of the poison pass more quickly through the bowel.

'Now I put him on oxygen, hyperventilate him and send him upstairs, don't I, Lester?'

His patient smiled but Pete knew it could be some time before signs of shock set in, with hypotension becoming more marked in twenty-four to forty-eight hours. He'd known patients suffer delayed cardiovascular complications four or five days later. Wondered again at the extremes to which some people sank.

'Aren't there new cyclic antidepressants which have fewer side-effects in overdose these days?' Anna asked, as they gathered up discarded packaging off the floor and set the room to rights.

'Three or four,' he replied, 'but perhaps they haven't been effective in treating Lester.'

'Where Tofranil has?' Anna's eyebrow climbed and he had to smile at the disgust in her voice.

'Wouldn't be a psychiatrist for quids, would you?'

She shook her head, then returned his smile. 'No,' she said, her voice saddened by the thought of the struggle those specialists had with chronically depressed patients.

They walked out to see the waiting room had filled up while they'd worked on Lester. Carol, on triage today, had a stack of files waiting for them on the front desk.

'Full house,' Pete said, taking the top file and glancing at it before passing it to Anna.

'But no one lying on the floor,' she pointed out, heading towards the cubicle where her patient would be waiting.

He took the next file, the next patient, and worked through the list, passing her occasionally, checking on her less often, but always aware of her presence in the department.

Was she aware of his?

'No, Mrs Simons, you don't have to come back tomorrow,' he assured his final patient, as she returned to the cubicle after an enema had proved successful. 'But get that script filled at the pharmacy and take one sachet of the medicine every day with your breakfast—mix it with juice if you like.'

Mrs Simons blessed him and waddled off, waving cheerfully to the staff who knew her from her regular visits. She'd be back in a month but who was he to alter her habits of a lifetime? There was probably some deep-seated inhibition or phobia to explain her chronic constipation, but no one else had managed to cure it and he doubted he would either.

'Does everyone in town keep their medical woes until Monday afternoon?' Anna asked him as they were walking out to their cars a little later.

'Mondays, generally,' he explained. 'Unless it's urgent, why ruin the weekend sitting around in a hospital waiting room? Much better to leave it until Monday—it often means you can take a sickie as well. No problems?'

She shook her head, then smiled—but not at him. Bill was lounging by her car.

'Didn't want to disturb you at work so I thought I'd wait here,' he said, then he glanced at his watch. 'And I'd speak to your boss about the hours he works you. You should have been out of there half an hour ago.'

'Tonight's an early night,' she told him, still smiling at him as if he were the cat's whiskers. Which he wasn't, as Pete knew.

'You drove me home so you know where I live, but I was too bowled over by your charm and beauty to get your phone number.'

Pete made a gagging noise and muttered, 'Too bowled over by my good red wine!'

He considered walking away, letting them chat in peace.

Didn't!

Why should he? It was a public car park after all!

'How about dinner tonight?' Bill asked, ignoring Pete so pointedly he found himself answering.

'Sorry, mate, no can do tonight. Maybe tomorrow.'

But it didn't make Anna laugh—in fact, the feeble joke made her look uncomfortable.

'I'm sorry, Bill,' she said, 'but we've a house rule at home which prohibits any of us going out week nights. Too many other things to do, and too hard on the system when the kids have school next day and I have work.'

She unlocked her car and Pete knew he should move away, give the pair a chance to talk alone. Forced his legs to lift his feet, his arm to lift his hand in a casual salute, and somehow made it to his car, unlocked the door, climbed in.

Don't look at them, his head warned, but he did, and felt heat flare in his body as Bill bent his head and kissed Anna—on the cheek.

Didn't do much for the simmering anger he was feeling—cheeks were far too close to lips. Considered her lips, so mobile—so damn kiss-able.

The thought stunned him.

No, he wasn't thinking of her like that. His concern over a developing relationship with Bill was because he suspected Bill wasn't right for her. Not a good role model for Josh either, if he took it further. No, he was certain Josh wouldn't approve of Bill any more than he did. He'd have to think of something to stop this before it went any further. Find someone else for her.

Perhaps talk to Josh!

*   *   *

About Ken as well, he decided the following day when Anna excused herself during a lull in patients, announcing she was going to the staff canteen for lunch.

'Ken Riddell just phoned her,' Margie told Pete. 'Think there's something going on there?'

The woman was a magnet for undesirable types, he decided, although, to be fair, he hadn't heard anything derogatory about Ken— in fact, nothing but praise as far as his professionalism was concerned. The hospital grapevine had it the man was a natural in O and G.

A specialist in women's health, conditions and ailments! Did it, therefore, follow that he was a natural with women?

Remembered his car was due for a service and put Anna Crane completely out of his mind. Phoned the garage to arrange it, chatted for a while about slip differentials and other man stuff, then smiled. The garage he used regularly was between her place and the hospital. He could ask her to pick him up there in the morning and drop him back after work. Give him a chance to suss out how she felt about her two courtiers outside the confines of the hospital.

The afternoon pace heated up. A child on a bicycle had been struck by a car, suffering severe lacerations and a broken leg, worse injuries having been prevented by the helmet she'd been wearing, correctly for a change, when the accident occurred. He and Anna worked together, the ABC of airways, breathing and circulation attended to first, then X-raying the leg and splinting it into position to minimise further damage, packing it with ice to reduce swelling, elevating it, earning pats on the back from the orthopaedic surgeon called down to consult.

He agreed he couldn't do more at the moment with the skin so badly lacerated and left them picking pieces of gravel from the seeping wounds, flooding the areas with antiseptic solution and finally covering them with gauze.

'We'll have to admit her,' he explained to the anxious mother, while Kim passed her the chart, explaining they needed a signature for the admittance. The woman signed.

'The analgesic we've given her in the drip will probably make her sleepy,' Pete continued. 'Do you want to go home and organise things there, then come back later?'

The woman stared blankly at him.

'Come back later? Why should I do that?'

'To be with her when she wakes,' Anna said gently, reaching out and touching the woman on the shoulder. 'We can arrange for you to stay if it's convenient.'

'But she's not *my* child!' the woman said, and Pete knew Anna was as shocked as he'd been by the pronouncement. In fact, they'd provided treatment to the child, thinking this woman's consent was parental.

'And it wasn't my fault,' she added, making things a little clearer. 'She just shot out of the driveway of this house, straight across the footpath and into my car. I braked and swerved but there was nothing I could do. I had a bus behind me and the bus driver called the ambulance. There was no one home in the house where she'd been or at the house next door and the ambulance had arrived by then so I came with her. Her name's Naomi—she did tell me that much.'

She looked at Pete and tears began to stream down her cheeks.

'And by now my car's probably been stolen. I just remembered I left my keys in it.'

'Come and sit down, I'll get you a cup of something hot,' Anna said, ushering her out of the cubicle and towards the lounge. 'The ambulance driver will have alerted the police to the accident if the bus driver didn't. I'm sure they've got everything under control by now, including your car.'

Pete watched her go then picked up the chart from the foot of the gurney. Naomi Clarke—in Kim's writing so presumably she'd also taken the woman as the girl's mother. No address was filled in, Kim no doubt thinking the 'mother' would provide that later. He returned the chart to its place and wondered whether he should keep her down here until she was identified. Hated the thought of leaving the child on her own if chaos suddenly erupted in the form of an aggressive patient or multiple trauma accident.

Decided to go with Mrs Clarke's signature and let the orderlies wheel the child away. Hopefully, the police would soon arrive to sort things out—and the parents of the child wouldn't raise hell over treating her without consent!

The police were first, but unfortunately they knew no more than he did—in fact, he was one up on them as the woman whose car had hit Naomi was still in the hospital, being cosseted by Anna.

'We door-knocked the street,' the older policeman said. 'It's an area of older homes, quite substantial, not many children living there at all, and no young girls about ten to twelve. Is that the age you'd assume?'

Pete agreed with the age assumption and led the two men towards the lounge where Anna was guarding the now-distraught Mrs Clarke.

'It was so sudden,' she kept repeating, seemingly not comforted by the fact that the bus driver had seen the entire incident and confirmed her story of what had happened.

The knowledge that it wasn't your fault didn't stop the guilt, Pete realised, then looked up as Anna spoke.

'The girl was in the uniform of a St Mary's student,' she offered. 'Bloodied, of course, but my daughter did her primary schooling there so I recognised it. Perhaps the school—'

The younger of the two policemen was already speaking into a small device Pete assumed to be a two-way radio, presumably asking someone back at the office to contact the school.

'And she had a lot of trinkets in her pocket. They'll have been bagged and…' She hesitated and looked at Pete. 'I'm not sure what you do with patients' possessions. Would they go up to the ward with her and be put into safe-keeping there, or held here?'

'They're probably still in the trauma room,' he said. 'Later, they're passed to Admin for safe-keeping.'

Leaving Mrs Clarke with Carol, who'd come in for a coffee-break, they all trooped back to the trauma room where Kim was cleaning up. Anna picked up the plastic bag and handed it to the policeman who tipped the contents into his hand and whistled.

'They can't be real,' Anna protested, 'or she wouldn't own them. She's far too young.'

'To be wagging school or stealing?' the older man said, then he sighed. 'I hate this kind of thing.'

'A teacher from the school is on the way,' his colleague announced after another quiet consultation with his two-way. 'Once we've identified her, we can go from there.'

'Piece of cake,' Pete muttered under his breath, but he knew it wouldn't be. Any situation regarding minors was fraught with danger and St Mary's was a private school—expensive. Wealthy parents could cause as much trouble as poor ones—more if they were so inclined—and they could also afford better lawyers.

'Perhaps it won't be too bad,' Anna said, as if sensing the trend of his thoughts.

'Perhaps it'll be worse!' he countered grimly, an uneasy foreboding stirring in his guts.

And it began by being worse when a tall, rumpled-looking man strode into the emergency room, spotted Anna and greeted her with unabashed delight, actually lifting her off the ground and swinging her around in the air before plonking her back down and kissing her soundly—on the lips, not the cheek!

Not at all the kind of behaviour he expected in his department. And he'd tell her so, first opportunity he got.

And he'd definitely speak to Josh. She obviously knew enough men, without him adding more of them to her list of conquests.

He made a hash of the man's name when she introduced him because he was thinking of other things—called him Drake, which was his surname as it turned out. His first name was Ben, he worked out later—a ridiculous name for a grown man, anyway.

'We've admitted her to the children's ward. I'll take you up,' Anna offered.

Pete glanced around—no patients for a change—and decided he'd go with them. Squeezed into the lift with a cluster of change-of-shift nurses, near Anna not Ben, regretted it immediately as her perfume did its 'wafting up his nose' thing again and distracted him into thoughts not purely medical.

'Apart from immobilising the leg and cleaning the wound, we haven't undertaken any treatment. I think the Naomi part is right. She gave that name to Mrs Clarke—I doubt she'd have made it up.'

Ben groaned.

'Naomi Bloody Wilson—bet your life it's the right name. It's not her fault, poor kid. You have to blame the parents.'

The lift doors opened and Anna ushered him out.

'Naomi Wilson—Nigel and Lexie Wilson's daughter?'

'The same,' Ben muttered, then he turned to Pete. 'Have you heard of Wilson's Property Development—the people building the golf course and residential estate on the outskirts of town?'

'Those Wilsons? Jeez! Perhaps the baubles were her own,' he added to Anna, who explained to Ben about the jewellery they'd found in the girl's pockets.

The two policemen were waiting outside the curtains which had been drawn around the child's bed. Anna introduced the teacher, then she waited outside with Pete while the three men went in.

'It's her,' Ben confirmed when he emerged. 'The police will contact the family but I guess I should stay here with her until someone comes. They might be upset.'

'You don't sound too sure of that,' Pete said, and saw the other man shrug.

'My guess is they'll be more annoyed by being dragged away from work than by anything their darling daughter has done. It's a classic case of a kid wanting more attention from her parents. Happens with her all the time in school—bad grades, misbehaviour, anything to get them on the premises for a while, to make them take some notice of her.'

Pete saw Anna turn away, a suspicious sheen washing across her bright eyes.

'We can't alter people's lives,' he said, putting his arm around her shoulders when she'd said goodbye to Ben and was walking back towards the lift. Giving her a hug.

'Yes, but isn't it hard when a kid who, to all observers, has so much actually has so little of the things she needs—love, attention, companionship with her parents. She's an only child, Ben said. Poor little blighter.'

He could hardly scold her for taking this patient to her heart when he agreed with everything she said—only he felt anger not sorrow.

They travelled down in the lift together, knowing Naomi's future was out of their control, but silent, as if their depressing thoughts precluded conversation.

'They've built up again,' she said, when they entered the waiting room together, but two of the multitude weren't patients. Janice Jennings and the bikie—Tim?

'Janice wants to talk to you,' Tim announced, looming over Anna but smiling to dissipate any sense of intimidation.

Janice actually looked as if she'd prefer to be anywhere but right here, but she stepped forward bravely. As Pete headed towards a cubicle to tackle the next patient he gathered that Anna had been right—true love had been blossoming between this unlikely couple and Tim plus dog were about to move into Janice's house.

'No reason why her father should be living there while she cowers in some shelter,' Tim growled, loudly enough for both Pete and all the waiting patients to hear. 'Mind, he can live there if he wants, but he'll have to watch himself. He so much as looks out of order at her, and I'll have him.'

He pounded his wounded hand into his palm and Pete smiled as he realised that here, at least, was a problem which had found its own solution.

He was still smiling as he entered the cubicle and greeted the man sitting, hunched over, on the examination table. Severe abdominal pain—not appendicitis but colicky pains possibly symptomatic of irritable bowel syndrome, he decided, listening to the rumbling sounds from the patient's lower abdomen.

'My GP's been at me for ages to have some tests,' his patient admitted. 'In fact, I've got a referral to a specialist in my wallet but I've been too busy.'

Pete ran through the man's medical history, paying particular attention to allergies and any indications of glaucoma, explaining that anticholinergic drugs were contraindicated in such cases.

'No to everything. This is the only thing I've ever had wrong with me,' the patient protested, 'and years ago I had a colonoscopy which didn't find anything to cause it. My GP gave me some tablets to take regularly, then I ran out and it started up again, hence the referral.'

'Which you didn't follow up. So now you're here, in agony, forced to take time off from work,' Pete pointed out. 'Can you remember what tablets you took. Were they Cantil?'

His patient grinned.

'No idea. My wife used to get them for me and hand them to me before meals, even tuck one in my lunch-box. I'm the original hopeless, helpless male in her view.'

'Did they make you drowsy, do you remember?'

'Not noticeably. I took them three times a day and still drove the car, things like that.'

'OK,' Pete said. 'I'm going to give you one of these now to relax the spasms, then you can rest here for a couple of hours. If you're feeling better then, and promise faithfully to go see the specialist soon, I'll let you go.'

He sent Carol for the drug and water, then left the cubicle, knowing there were more patients waiting, more pain behind the curtains which moved gently as he walked along the corridor for the next file.

'I've a woman I think is in premature labour,' Anna said, appearing from behind a curtain and falling in beside him. 'Do we treat her here or send her straight upstairs?'

'How premature?' he asked.

'Eighteen weeks give or take.'

'Phone O and G to alert them and send her up. By the time we get the drugs she'll need to slow the labour, we can have her up there with the experts.'

She nodded and disappeared again. Seconds later he heard the gurney wheels roll towards the lift, knew she'd be phoning while the woman was on her way—pleased again that she worked effectively, which wasn't always the same as efficiently.

He must remember to tell her he was pleased, he thought, then recalled the school teacher greeting her and why he wasn't pleased, snapped at Margie when she repeated a question and, shame-faced, headed for the cubicle where his next patient waited.

A badly crushed and mangled toe attached—but only just—to a belligerent-looking ten-year-old.

'How did it happen?' he asked, noting the vital signs Joanne had already taken.

'Not telling,' the child replied, glaring at the other adult who hovered by the bed.

'OK,' Pete said easily, and introduced himself to the woman, checking she was the mother, and that, yes, he could do whatever he liked to young Robert, preferably murder him.

'He put it under the car tyre, that's what he did to it. It's a wonder he didn't crush his entire foot. Sat there on the drive with his toe propped under the tyre, then got his brother to take the car out of gear and roll it forward. Wanted to see if it would hurt. His brother will be grounded for the rest of his life and if you'd keep this one in hospital until he's twenty-one, I'd be very grateful.'

Pete chuckled. The woman had every reason to be fed up, but he could hear the fondness and anxiety beneath her crossness and wished young Naomi had someone who cared for her as much.

'It will need reconstructive surgery to get it operating even partially again.' He turned to the phone, hoping one of the surgeons who specialised in microsurgery was still in the building. The sooner the delicate stitching and piecing together began, the more chance there was for a successful outcome.

'Send him up,' the sister in Children's Surgical said. 'We'll pass him on to Theatre from here.'

Joanne summoned help and Pete explained to Robert's mother why they wanted to get on to it straight away.

'Why don't you go up with him and speak to Sister? She'll be able to give you some idea of how long he'll be in Theatre.'

'They will be able to fix it?' she asked, and he saw the worry in her eyes.

'Once those fellows up there finish with it, it will be almost as good as new. You a soccer player, Robert? Need that toe?'

The lad nodded then reached out and took his mother's hand as orderlies appeared to take him upstairs.

Not such a tough kid after all!

'We're really shuffling them in and up this afternoon,' Anna commented, watching as another of her patients was transported upstairs. 'Does it always happen like this? Some days minor stuff that we stitch or dress then send home, and other days when everyone comes to stay?'

'There's no pattern to it,' Pete admitted, wondering if she was feeling tired, the way she rubbed her neck, slipping her hand beneath her hair to massage the skin. Wondering how the skin would feel! Silky smooth? How heavy that mass of hair? 'Nights and weekends are more predictable, which reminds me—I know you must have been asked about your availability for night and weekend work when you were interviewed, but—'

'You'd been on duty thirty-six hours straight—the medical super explained that to me when you drifted off to sleep. And to answer your question, yes, I'm available for normal rostering any time, day or night.'

'What about the children?' he asked, and her eyes lit up with an impish glee.

'Don't ever let Josh hear you call him a child,' she warned. 'His teenage sensitivities couldn't cope.' Her smile faded and she added seriously, 'They're very independent and capable. We talked about it before I applied for the job, how they'd manage. Josh is content to be in charge at home if I'm working nights or weekends, and Jackie obeys him—most of the time—so there'll be no more trouble between them than the normal sibling friction.'

'They're not perfect?' Pete teased, wanting to see her eyes sparkle again.

'No, thank goodness,' she said. 'Perfect would worry me to death, always wondering when the crash was coming. Give me normal any day.'

She looked into his eyes, her own questioning.

'Are you doing rosters that you're asking? I thought I was fixed on days for three months.'

'I'm not, and you are,' he replied, wondering why that steady gaze of hers should make his bowels clench. 'I was simply wondering about the kids—I suppose because we've had a few come through today.'

'Like Naomi Wilson—a latchkey kid. One of the reasons I was so long returning to work was that I felt I couldn't do that to Jackie and Josh while they were younger. They needed to know someone was there for them all day every day—for a while—until things settled down and their confidence in my place in their life grew stronger.'

He stared at her, wondering if most women would think that way. But, then, most women wouldn't have married a dying man to give his children security.

Had she loved him?

He guessed she'd have had to love him to have done what she had.

Wanted to ask.

Knew it wasn't his business.

Asked about a lift to work instead, feeling foolish because it seemed so trivial. Even more foolish when he was pleased she said yes.

CHAPTER SIX

NEXT day, Anna not only collected Pete from the garage where he'd left his car, but returned him to it later that evening. The place was closed, his big four-wheel drive sitting in the shadows.

'Will they have left the keys somewhere?' she asked as he climbed out of her sedan.

He bent down and waved a spare key at her. 'They'll be locked inside. I'm invariably late collecting it.'

'This late?' she asked, glancing at her watch.

He knew it was close to nine. They'd been working on the victims of a small commuter bus accident when the new shift began, and had stayed until everyone had been treated.

'Sometimes,' he admitted, wondering why he didn't straighten up and walk away.

'You're not far from my place now—why not come over and have a quick bite to eat? The kids will have heated a casserole for dinner and there'll be leftovers sitting in the oven, waiting for me to reheat them.'

He knew he should say no but heard himself muttering something to the effect that it *would* save him getting dinner for himself.

After all, he justified to himself as he followed her car up the hill towards the big house, it would also give him a chance to report on his progress to Josh.

The house oozed the same kind of welcome it had last time he'd visited, the two kids loud in their appreciation of his company. He waited until Anna was in the big kitchen organising their meal and Jackie had returned to her homework, then mentioned Bill to Josh—had they met him?

'Sure, he's cool,' Josh assured him. 'Great guy. He's taking me out on his jet-ski on Sunday—Jackie, too, if she wants to come but she reckons jet-skis are too big and noisy for her so she'll probably hang around on the beach with Anna.'

Knew he shouldn't ask—that it wasn't any of his business. Heard the words. 'You're *all* going with him on Sunday?'

'Yes, out to the lake. It's still quite warm so it should be a bit of fun.'

'Yes, I go there myself occasionally but I'm into quieter pursuits, like windsurfing—not those huge noisy jet-ski things.'

He hadn't been out to the lake for months and wasn't certain where he'd stacked his sails when he'd moved into the town-house, but he half hoped Josh might suggest he join them.

Almost got his wish.

'I suppose you could come along,' the lad said—not exactly delighted at the prospect if his voice was any indication. 'But it might be best to leave Anna and Bill together on their own for a bit. Jackie and I had already decided we'd take a long hike around the foreshore. And, by the way, I've been meaning to thank you.' He beamed at Pete. 'I didn't think you'd come up with anyone this quickly—and to find two really great blokes for her to choose from, well, that's OTT.'

Pete stared at the hair, the eyebrow ring, and realised Josh had absolutely no taste. He, Pete, should have known that from the start—and he definitely couldn't rely on him to sort out who was acceptable as a suitor for Anna. Really great blokes? Spare me!

'OTT,' he echoed faintly, grappling with the shock caused by Josh's enthusiasm for both Ken and Bill.

'Over the top,' Josh translated obligingly, then he clapped Pete on the shoulder, muttered something about hitting the books and disappeared.

'I hope he hasn't been bothering you.' Anna's voice brought him back to earth. 'I think he enjoys having a man to talk to.'

Aren't Bill and Ken enough? he wanted to demand, but this time his mouth refused to work and the words were stifled, caught up in his head like the echo of a bad dream.

He sat down at the table, took the plate and cutlery she offered him, and felt his taste-buds spring to life as the delicious aroma rose to tempt them.

'This is leftover casserole?' he asked, trying it to see if it was as good as it smelt. It was.

Anna smiled at his obvious enjoyment.

'We have a big cooking day about once a month. All three of us in the kitchen, making different dishes to pack into the freezer. Josh's speciality is spaghetti sauce, his own secret recipe that I suspect changes each time he makes it—but it always tastes good and it's an easy meal for the kids to fix for themselves when I'm not home.'

'Which is nearly every evening.'

She glanced up at him as if surprised by his words.

'No. I've only been late once or twice so far, although I know times like today could happen more often. Jackie and Josh have a good feed when they get home from school and that holds them through to about eight o'clock for dinner...'

She was still talking but he'd lost the thread, too busy picturing them here at the big table— eating and talking together, relating the details of their various days. Though why he, who'd never hankered after domesticity, should find it appealing, he didn't know.

The talk drifted back to shop, and his battle to keep the A and E department—sorry, Rod, emergency room—a viable functioning unit.

'Airlifting patients to bigger centres for specialist treatment is all very well,' he explained when she questioned why he was so determined on this subject. 'And I accept for spinal injuries and bad burns it makes sense to have them in a specialist unit, but transferring patients disrupts the entire family or leaves the patient without the support of those closest to him or her—the very factors which can make an enormous difference in the patient's will to live, his or her determination to fight.'

'So we keep whoever we can?' she teased. 'Cling to them and guard them jealously?'

'Do I sound demented about it? I'm sorry, it's a hobby-horse of mine.'

She reached across the table and patted his hand, as casually as if he'd been one of her stepchildren.

'Don't apologise. It's great to hear conviction. Too many people go with the flow these days, content to let someone else do the fighting. It's the ''I'm all right, Jack'' syndrome, isn't it?'

Her hand had felt so cool—so soft—yet that platonic touch had provoked heat, not coolness, a tensing of his muscles, not a relaxation. He tried to think of something to say but his saliva had dried up—the mega-mouth had finally run out of words.

'I should be off,' he managed, knew it to be true—right now, before he made a fool of himself and did a little touching of his own. It was because her skin appeared so white in the shaded light of the verandah—like marble, cool and smooth. Would it feel like stone? Or like a flesh-and-blood woman?

Sat there like a dummy, his assertion hanging in the air between them, thought of something else he wanted to say. What about your first husband? None of your business, she might tell him, which, of course, would only make him more eager to know—more intrigued. Perhaps he'd ask Josh.

'I'll give you a hand with the dishes first.'

That was better—a reasonable excuse to linger a little longer in her company.

'I put them in the dishwasher,' she said. 'It's no bother—two plates, two knives, two forks and a casserole dish. Not beyond my capabilities.' She was smiling at him as she spoke, teasing him as he suspected she did most of the time.

'I doubt there's much that is,' he said, and saw the widening of her eyes, the startled look.

Good! She surprised him often enough—it was time he shook her a little.

But it broke the peace between them. She stood up, sketched a little bow and said pertly, 'Why, thank you, kind sir.'

Then she moved lightly away towards the kitchen, calling back over her shoulder, 'Would you like coffee? I'm sorry, I didn't think to ask earlier. I try not to drink too much of it at night.'

Which was as good as saying he'd be a nuisance if he said yes—if he stayed.

Found himself wanting to say yes if only to annoy her. It couldn't be because he wanted to stay, could it? He was still considering the pros and cons when he heard Jackie call to her.

'Homework problem,' Anna relayed to him, poking her head around the kitchen door. 'The coffee might be a while.'

He stood up, refused coffee, thanked her for the meal and explained he should have left ages ago, making it sound as if he had things to do, places to go, people to see, and this dalliance had severely disrupted his timetable.

'Can you find your way out?' she asked. 'Or should I see you to your car? Make sure you don't get lost?'

That teasing smile again, but Jackie was waiting and there was moonlight outside. Much better she didn't see him to his car. His body was in enough chaos without moonlit red hair thrown in to the equation.

'I'll find my way,' he assured her, and did just that, but he wasn't certain as he drove away if he *had* found his way—or if he'd suddenly lost it completely.

He slept badly again, got up early and went to work, arriving as Anna pulled into the car park.

'You're worse than I am,' he grumbled, 'coming in before you're due to start.'

'I kept thinking of all the follow-up work on that bus accident. I doubt if half the admission forms would have GPs' names or addresses, and when we left the police were still hunting up relatives. I thought there might be something I could do.'

'Me, too,' he agreed, smiling now, pleased by her dedication—pleased to see her, if the truth be told.

'I've also had an idea.' She blurted out the words and the look she gave him showed how tentative she felt in broaching it.

'Tell me as we walk,' he suggested, taking her elbow and guiding her across the acres of bitumen.

'Well...'

'Come on, I don't bite.'

She turned to him, smiled, then shook her head so the curls fluttered in the early morning light like a cloud of red butterflies—or was it dragonflies he meant?

'Well,' she began again, less tentatively this time, 'you know how most of the people we see in A and E, apart from the accidents, are folk who don't have regular check-ups, no GP, not under treatment at Outpatients.'

'People who leave things until they are so sick they can't put off a visit any longer—yes, you've about summed them up. I've always believed if we could persuade them to make regular visits they'd be healthier, we'd be less busy and health-care costs would drop.'

'That's what I'm talking about—maintenance stuff like we do on our cars. In fact, it was you taking your car to the garage yesterday which made me think about it.'

They'd reached the doors and he held her back, knowing that the moment they walked into the department they might not have time to talk.

'And?'

Another searching look. Checking to see if he was taking her seriously?

'I wondered about the hospital staff. I know from the information I was given when I applied for the job that hospital staff are welcome to use the outpatients facility, but is there any plan of regular health checks? You must know yourself that doctors are the worst when it comes to fobbing off an ache or pain until it becomes too late.'

'Your late husband?' he asked, and saw her nod.

'But he was only one,' she said. 'We tend to preach healthy living but do we practise it? How much exercise do you get? I know I tell myself I'm on my feet all day, running from one cubicle to the next, but is it the same as regular planned and programmed exercise?'

'It's a good idea, Anna, possibly a great idea, but there's a gym in the hospital and a staff pool in the grounds, and I doubt staff get much time to use either. When they're off duty they want to be out of here.'

She nodded, but he saw determination in the tilt of her chin and knew he'd hear more of this. However, if Anna was about to embark on a campaign for a healthier staff, she'd have an uphill task. Most health professionals considered they knew enough to take care of themselves, although her observations had been right—few practised what they preached.

The next he heard about her idea was in a department heads' meeting the following day, Friday. It had been a busy week but not that busy. In fact, if he faced the truth, he'd been avoiding her. Checked routinely on her work, as he would with any junior, but dodged opportunities to be alone with her, put her off when she suggested they talk, used excuses about end-of-month pressures and a backlog of paperwork.

So, to have the medical super raving on about pre-emptive health care, not just for the medical and support staff but also for the catering, housekeeping and grounds staff, was something of a shock.

Alan Carr, the MS, glanced across the room at Pete and nodded in appreciation. 'The idea came out of the emergency department, and was prompted by the fact that most of the chronic illness and out-of-control disease they see is in patients who could and should have been treated earlier—things a regular health-care programme would have picked up on and at least treated if not cured.'

Pete clenched his teeth, accepting the praise with his silence, sorry he hadn't listened to more details of Anna's idea, wondering why she'd included him in the presentation of it when he'd so assiduously avoided discussing it with her.

Wondering why neither of her husbands had murdered her.

'We can't force the outside population to accept a regular programme of health checks, but we can, as Drs Jackson and Crane suggest, ask staff to attend regular clinics—free of charge, of course—and have blood-pressure, choles-terol and blood tests,' Alan continued. 'We will treat whatever is treatable and give advice on healthier living, exercise, weight loss, and so on. In a hospital this size we have the personnel with the expertise in our ancillary staff—dietitians, physio and occupational therapists—to provide all these things, but do we make enough use of what's available ourselves?'

It was a rhetorical question—not that Pete had been about to answer. Anna had already done that for him in her submission. Alan was now rabbiting on about instituting the programme, asking David what times Outpatients was least busy, what extra staff he'd need for the initial checks, how he saw it working best.

And David, rot his soul, was sounding equally enthusiastic, positively beaming at the thought of the extra work or was it the thought of finally being involved in a programme of preventative medicine that he was happy about?

We should all be happy about it, he realised. It was the way good, effective health care should work.

So why wasn't he pleased?

The answer was waiting back in the Emergency Room, obviously twitchy with anticipation. Alan must have told her the suggestion would come up at the meeting.

Pete deliberately ignored the subject, asking first if there was a patient she wished him to see, then heading for his office when she said, no, it had been very quiet.

He knew he'd upset her, walking away like that, but he had to sort out his own feelings— work out why he was annoyed—before he could talk to her. Decided, after long cogitation, that it was because he knew the amount of work she must have put into the submission—extra work on top of the long hours she worked here.

But as long as she did her job efficiently why should he care?

Considered it for a while, then decided no amount of thinking was going to solve the puzzle and shelved it, picking up the copy of the letter she'd sent to Alan—a copy he remembered seeing on his desk on Wednesday.

He finally emerged to find her busy with a three-week-old infant who'd presented with projectile vomiting, already dehydrated, the mother hysterical about her baby boy.

'He cries with hunger after he's been sick then this happens again when I feed him.' The mother was sobbing out her distress to Kim, who was comforting her while Anna, standing on the infant's left, gently palpated the baby's abdomen.

She glanced up as if she knew Pete had come into the cubicle and motioned him over.

'I can remember learning about feeling a small lump like an olive in cases of pyloric stenosis, and I'm certain I can feel one here. Would you like to check it?'

She stood aside and he put his hands on the infant's legs to raise them as he gently felt the abdomen.

Nodded to Anna, who turned to the woman, explaining how sometimes the pyloric sphincter, at the outlet of the stomach, was too tight and failed to release food into the intestine.

'The surgeons perform a very simple operation under light anaesthesia,' she said, again glancing at Pete for confirmation. He nodded and she continued. 'They cut some muscle fibres to widen the opening, and the little fellow will be as good as new in no time.'

'He'll have to stay in hospital?' the woman asked, and this time Anna took over at the table, waving Pete aside while she re-dressed the baby with neat, efficient movements, leaving him to answer.

'The paediatric surgeon will tell you that. I'd assume it will be overnight after the operation,' he said. 'Dr Crane will make the arrangements for you.'

But Dr Crane seemed to have forgotten she was supposed to be admitting a patient. She'd picked up the now swaddled infant and was holding him up, cooing at him in a most undoctorly fashion, talking to him as if he understood exactly what she was saying—making Pete uncomfortable with this display of maternalism.

Most uncomfortable. Physically so.

He went back to his office to have another think!

Buzzed Margie and asked her if she'd send Anna into him when she was free.

She came five minutes later, smiling happily, as if pleased to be spending time with him—or perhaps because her diagnosis had proved correct. That would be more likely.

He was about to greet her when the phone rang. Waved her to a chair and picked up.

Cousin Liz, quacking on in his ear.

'Hey, slow down, let me get this straight. You're catering for a cocktail party to launch what? Yes, I suppose I can come if you're sure you need support, though what good I'd be at something like that, I don't know. It will be all women.'

'It won't,' Liz argued. 'Most salons are owned by men even if they're run by women. And I don't want you buying—I want you there because I'm nervous and need someone on my side in the crowd. Just to be there for me.'

He sighed and she chuckled.

'Don't do the martyr bit, Pete, it doesn't suit you. Not so long ago you'd have leapt at the chance to meet a bunch of gorgeous young women. You're getting stodgy—misogynous, your mother says. Hey, why don't you ask Anna if she'd like to come along? I think she'd find it fun.'

He glanced across the table at the subject of the conversation. She was reading a medical journal she'd picked up off his desk, studiously avoiding listening to his conversation—trying to pretend she wasn't there.

'Liz has to cater for a cocktail party tomorrow night. Needs a bit of moral support as she's still new at the job. Wondered if you'd like to go along. It's a launch of some hair stuff.'

Her face lit up with pleasure.

'Not the new Rombeau range?'

He repeated the question to Liz, who affirmed it was indeed the very latest thing in hair care, but his mind lingered on Anna's reaction. Could a woman who thought and reacted like a man—when she was at work—still get excited about hair-care products, for heaven's sake?

Nodded to her and saw her nod back. Their heads would fall off if they kept this up.

'She'd like to go,' he said to Liz. 'What time and where?'

'Six o'clock at the Old Mill,' Liz told him. 'See you both there.'

Anna was positively glowing when he passed on this information and once again he realised that the gulf between men and women was unbridgeable. He could imagine getting reasonably excited about a game of golf with Greg Norman, but hair-care products?

'Thanks so much for organising that for me,' Anna said as he replaced the receiver. 'I'd seen an ad for it, but thought it was closed to the general public.'

He saw a faint pinkness tinge her cheeks and her eyes take on a kind of shy look. Intriguing, that shy look—more alluring than usual!

'I've never bothered much with that kind of thing,' she admitted. 'I mean, I couldn't afford it when I was growing up or studying, then later, with intern years and first residencies, there was no time to think of anything personal. But recently, when the kids suggested I try a new hair colour, something brighter than my natural mouse...'

Her colour had deepened and he felt a rush of warmth towards her, this woman who was embarrassed by what to her was a new interest in how she looked—or how her hair looked, anyway. Most of the women he knew had been interested in how their hair looked since they were five—his sisters included.

Found himself pleased to be able to please her.

'It starts at six. Shall I collect you at a quarter to or would you prefer to be fashionably late?'

Now she stared at him, seeming as flustered and confused as if he'd lapsed into Swahili. Frowned mightily, then said hesitantly, 'You're going, too?'

What did she think?

'She's my cousin and she needs support. Of course I'm going.'

The flush became a blush and she stammered a few confused sentences about any time would suit her, then she stood up and walked out of the room.

Which was probably just as well as he'd completely forgotten what he'd wanted to discuss with her. For some reason, his mind had been diverted by that colour in her cheeks, wondering if she'd look flushed and pink when she was making love. Knew it would have to be himself in the act with her or he wouldn't ever know.

Fantasising about sex with his 'team'?

Impossible!

Maybe he needed a holiday—a long holiday.

Was called into a patient instead—another child, eighteen months old. Even before Pete reached the cubicle he could hear the paroxysm of coughs followed by the higher-pitched inhalation as the child struggled for air to refill the lungs.

'He was tired, listless, a bit off his food last week, but no sign of anything else. Then today this started. He goes blue each time he coughs. I didn't know what to do.'

Wendy waited until the next burst of coughing finished then placed an oxygen mask over the child's mouth and nose.

'I'll take a swab to confirm it but I'd say it's pertussis—whooping cough. And a bad dose, the poor little blighter,' he added when the child began to cough again as the air escaped from his lungs. 'Has he been immunised?'

Silly question. The child wouldn't be fully immune until the course was completed when he was five—and it was now he was suffering.

'Yes, he has,' the woman stated firmly.

'Well, it may be a less severe bout than he'd have had otherwise,' Pete reassured her, wondering if perhaps Anna's scheme of regular health checks for hospital staff could extend to immunisation of their children. Must mention it to someone.

'I'll put him on a course of antibiotics, which will help reduce contagiousness and perhaps prevent any complications, but the infection has to run its course unfortunately. He needs lots of rest, plenty of liquids and normal meals. If you can keep him away from pollutants like dust or smoke, which might aggravate his lungs, and keep him as quiet as possible, he'll get better more quickly.'

He waited while she considered this, studying the information Wendy had gathered on admission—the child's pulse and respiratory rate, family background.

'We could keep him in here for a few days, if that would be better,' he suggested. Four other children in the house wasn't his idea of a restful environment. 'It would isolate him from your other children in case they haven't already picked up the infection, and also allow us to help him over the worst with oxygen and suction, as well as nursing staff to keep an eye on him.'

The mother studied her little boy, lying still at the moment, his skin pale, limbs limp from the exertion of coughing. Then she frowned as if the decision was too much for her.

'He'd be better here but I couldn't get up to visit much, except at night when the others have gone to bed.'

Pete nodded.

'We could try it, and if he gets upset being here on his own we could work out something else. Can you go up with him while the ward staff settle him in? Is there someone minding your other children?'

The woman began to cry, quietly sniffing into her handkerchief.

'Mum is. She's the one who said he should go to hospital—said it was whooping cough, but I didn't believe her. Kids don't get that kind of thing these days, I said, and look at him.'

Pete looked instead at the young woman, saw the tiredness beneath her worry and wondered how she coped with the domestic juggling of five children and a husband. Plenty did, he knew that—his mother had handled six kids—but when he saw women like this one he understood just what a toll it took of them at times.

'Perhaps your mother could stay overnight with the other children and you could be here with Donny. There's special accommodation for the parents of sick children. Your husband could join you here. We wouldn't expect you to spend the night by his bed, but you could use the little bedsitting room and the staff could call you if he woke and was fretful.'

The woman looked doubtful, then hopeful, then a smile as bright as a lottery winner's lit up her face.

'A night on our own? Would we have to pay for it?'

Pete shook his head, watching guilt and hope vie in her face as she considered this treat then worried about enjoying something that was a direct result of her child's illness.

'Go upstairs with Donny, speak to Sister and tell her I suggested you stay. If it's OK with her, phone your mother.' He patted her on the shoulder, remembered the new 'rules' about touching patients or their relatives even in sympathy, decided they were nonsense in this situation and patted her again.

'Don't feel guilty. He may well need you, and you could easily spend the night nursing him, but at least you'll have your husband with you and you won't have to be worrying about his coughing waking the other kids.'

She managed a watery smile and left with Wendy and an orderly who'd come down from the children's ward with a gurney.

He watched them go, and realised he was finished for the day when he saw Phil from the evening shift sitting at their shared desk.

'Not a lolly or a biscuit left in any drawer—I checked,' Phil grumbled. 'I used to like taking over from you because you always had a few little sugar boosters stashed away. What's happening? A special romantic interest in your life? Mind on sex, not carbohydrates? Now, if it was your new ''team'' I'd understand your distraction, but the grapevine has it the recent addition to the O and G staff has snaffled her. So what gives? Where are the sweeties?'

He winked lewdly—as if Pete mightn't get the double meaning.

Pete scowled at him.

'If I spent less time running this department and more time exercising, I'd be glad to keep

the place stocked with treats, but right now I'm
flat out at work and my sister Jill tells me I'm
developing a paunch.'

Phil roared with laughter and Pete cuffed
him lightly on the shoulder.

'It's all right for you to laugh, youngster,'
he grouched, 'but this exercise stuff gets serious when you're heading for forty.'

Although *he* hadn't taken it seriously, he
realised later when he'd said goodbye to Phil
and was walking towards his car. And he'd
laughed off Jill's suggestion. Until now.

Now he was seriously considering a trip to
the lake on Sunday—to go windsurfing, nothing more. That was the best exercise he knew
for stomach muscles. He could drive beyond
the places where most people went, find a se-
cluded spot and spend some time alone—pit-
ting himself against the wind and water.

It had been moving into the town-house that
had been the problem, finding furniture after
living in furnished flats for so long, getting the
plants around the courtyard established, doing
domestic stuff. He'd let his leisure activities
slip—his social life, too, for that matter.

And all he had to look forward to this week-end on the social scene was a cocktail party to launch some new hair product.

With a woman who'd seemed put out that he was taking her.

Great!

CHAPTER SEVEN

IF PETE had given the dress-code business any serious thought he'd have realised what the words 'cocktail party' signified in terms of women's attire. As a man, he had no problems with deciding what to wear. Shorts or jeans to all casual functions at weekends, casual trousers and a sports jacket to weekday casual, a suit to funerals or official hospital functions like grand openings and his monkey suit to the hospital ball and the occasional fancy wedding.

A cocktail party at which he was to support his cousin in her new business venture said suit to him so he arrived at Anna's house, the staid grey of his suit enlivened by a bright tie. Hairdresser types had a tendency towards flamboyance and he didn't want to appear out of place.

Jackie greeted him, asked him inside—to the formal sitting room this time, not the back

170

verandah—offered him a drink and explained Anna wouldn't be long.

Josh drifted in, a soft drink in one hand and a tennis ball in the other.

'You ever do much weights?' he asked, squeezing the tennis ball as he spoke, watching his muscles move, not looking at Pete.

'When I was at school—on the rowing team. We did a lot in off-season training. Routines designed to build up the quads and shoulders.'

Josh nodded and drifted off again, saying, 'Thought so.' He disappeared out of sight.

High heels clicked across the polished wooden floors, and a vision appeared. Now—too late—he remembered all the things he'd learned about cocktail parties back when he'd lived at home with his sisters. Remembered they gave women licence to wear the skimpiest of garments—mere scraps of material which left inordinate amounts of leg and skin show-ing. Not that he could see bare leg—oh, no, that was slinkily, and sneakily, covered with sheer black stockings.

'Wow!'

He wasn't certain whether he or Jackie spoke, but if it wasn't him it was exactly what he would have said.

'Wow!' Josh returned and put more emphasis into it. 'You'll knock 'em dead, stepmama,' he said fondly.

Pete stared at him, unable to believe what he was hearing. The lad should be reprimanding her, not praising her—telling her she shouldn't be going out looking like that.

She must have heard his silence for she twirled around in front of him, her aggravating eyebrow lifting as she silently asked for his approval to be added to the chorus.

Not that he could have answered if he'd wanted to. His spit had dried up. Hell, he'd heard of scared spitless, but this wasn't fear.

It wasn't?

Then why was his heart racing, blood pumping so fast through his veins he could hear the roar of it like an express train in his ears?

'He's stunned,' Jackie said kindly. 'Too used to seeing you in your work togs. Now, off you go, you two. Have a nice time, don't be late home and don't drink and drive.'

At any other time he'd have laughed at the youngster playing mother, but this wasn't any other time and he was struggling to find normal—doubting he'd be able to drive, even stone cold sober, with that dress and those legs in the car beside him.

Waited while Anna said goodbye to the two kids, made sure they had the phone number of the hotel, fussed a little over Jackie, then led the way out of the house.

'Shouldn't there be more of that dress?' he demanded when they were out of the teenagers' hearing range.

She spun towards him as quickly as if he'd physically reached out and turned her around.

'You don't like it? It looks too young for me? Too tarty? I did wonder myself but Jackie helped me choose it when I was going to something else, then Josh was sick and I didn't go and I haven't ever worn it. So this seemed like a good time, but when I put it on I did wonder. It's very short, isn't it, and perhaps a bit low cut?'

She hitched at the skirt, which moved an eighth of an inch lower on her thighs, then touched her hand to where the neckline revealed a slight swell of porcelain breasts, her face creased with concern, her eyes pleading for his input.

Not approval?

He stared at her.

No, this wasn't a woman seeking a compliment. That much was obvious to even the dimmest of dimwits—a classification he fitted quite neatly at the moment.

She was seriously disturbed about her appearance—about the dress—but more than that, about her judgement in matters of appearance. He'd have preferred to take her to this damn cocktail party in a pair of his old flannelette pyjamas, well covered from toes to chin, but that, it suddenly struck him, was his problem not hers.

He touched her cheek where the dimple usually resided and said, 'I believe the rule for cocktail parties is to wear as little as possible, for balls as much as possible. My sisters taught me that years ago, but I'd forgotten. I don't do the cocktail circuit much these days.'

Saw her smile, her radiance, and knew he'd managed—just—to retrieve the situation.

As far as she was concerned. For him, the old pyjamas still held appeal, or maybe the air-conditioning would be frigid and he could wrap her in his coat.

Opened the car door for her and as she climbed in he realised just how much leg would show beneath the coat and scrapped that idea. Very seductive—suggestive—a woman's legs appearing beneath the bottom of a man's suit coat. Black stockinged legs at that!

Swore quietly to himself as he made his way around to the driver's door. And as for drinking and driving—they could get a cab home. Right now, what he needed was a stiff Scotch.

You don't drink Scotch, the puritan in his head reminded him.

Well, maybe it's time I did, he replied, then he glanced towards his silent and still tentative partner, smelt the perfume she always wore, put the car into gear and went forwards instead of backwards, hitting her garage doors with a sickening crunch and bringing the two kids flying out of the house.

'We'll worry about the damage tomorrow,' Anna said calmly to the children, waving to them to go back inside the house. She turned to Pete. 'Do you want to check your car or is it tough enough to withstand these minor incidents?'

He stared at her, aware she'd regained her usual poise, aware he'd lost whatever of the same quality he'd ever had.

'The bull-bar will have taken the brunt of it but I'm sorry about your door. I'll have it fixed for you, of course.'

Drove off, feeling about seventeen when everything in the world used to conspire to embarrass him. Must talk to Josh about it one day. The lad didn't act like anything bothered him, but was it all a pose? Or perhaps Josh had gone though that awkward adolescent phase when he was younger? They say kids are maturing younger—

'I'm sorry, I was miles away,' he muttered, realising Anna was carrying on some form of polite conversation with him. Or perhaps it hadn't been polite conversation. Perhaps she'd been saying deep and meaningful stuff.

Glanced at her, saw her smiling at him and the way the red of the stoplight threw a blush across her breasts—chest—felt himself blushing again, thinking of sex, wondered about the need for experienced A and E practitioners in monasteries.

Caught the gist of the conversation—shop— a patient she'd seen and was concerned about. It kept them going all the way to the hotel, where his mind again went into denial and he wondered why he should care that the concierge took a sneak look at Anna's legs as she climbed out of the car.

Liz was ordering her minions around as they walked in, but she crossed the room to greet them, complimented Anna extravagantly and said, 'You can look after yourself, Pete, darling.' And promptly dragged Anna away to meet someone.

A male someone—many male someones, and not all of them dressed outrageously at all.

'They want to use me as a model,' Anna announced, returning to his side a little later and taking the champagne flute he'd snaffled for her from a passing waiter.

She gulped it down, looked into his eyes and said, 'For my hair—that's all. I didn't know what to say.'

Blue enough to drown in, her eyes were tonight. It must be the blue stuff lightly shadowing her eyelid, or the sneaky black lines she'd drawn along her lashes.

Or magic?

'Well, what did you tell them?' he demanded, realising he was going to be propping up a wall at this place all evening while she went off to have her hair fixed.

'I said I'd ask you,' she replied, managing to look both confused and adorable at the same time.

'Does it matter what I think?'

Too blunt, that question. Adorable disappeared, replaced by startled. And embarrassed?

'Yes,' she said simply. 'After all, I'm only here because you were kind enough to ask me, and if I go off and have my hair done you'll be on your own, and I know you can look after yourself and there are probably any number of gorgeous young women you're dying to meet, but I thought it would be rude—'

He held up his hand to stop the flow, ashamed of his dog-in-the-manger reaction when she'd only been considering him.

'Would you like to have your hair done?' he asked, and saw the colour seep up beneath her skin again.

'I think I would. I mean, I know about colour now, but I always seem to wear it out, just
flopping everywhere, or tied back, and I don't
know what else to do with it. I've only grown
it longer since I lived here in Huntley so I
don't understand how to put it up, apart from
gathering it untidily into a bunch with a clip—
and I've no idea what kind of look suits me.'

She gazed at him with the fixed attention of
a child who'd been offered a treat but wasn't
certain if she should accept. Was she really this
naïve? Twice married and excited about someone fiddling with her hair? His sisters had
spent most of their teenage years in the bathroom, fiddling with their own or each other's
hair. How come Anna had missed out?

'Go get your hair done, model-girl,' he said,
and saw the doubts vanish as a smile of sheer
delight lit up her face.

'But don't take it too seriously,' he warned
her. 'You know hairdressers. They might be
trying for extreme fashion, make you look like
Medusa. Your hair is great the way you wear
it.'

She looked surprised, as well she might. He
was pretty startled himself. Let her go and

found a waiter. Perhaps he'd have a glass of champagne after all. If he had one now, early in the evening—and just the one—it wouldn't affect his ability to drive home later.

He was rescued from the wall by a lively blonde, astute, flirtatious, the kind of woman who oozed self-confidence, whose mannerisms and body language told him she'd be interested in knowing him better—but not on a long-term basis.

And he should know—she was exactly the type of woman he'd enjoyed dalliances with since way back when he'd proposed to Kate and had been met by mirthful delight and told he wasn't ready for marriage yet. At least, not to someone like her who intended to make it stick once she took the plunge.

At the time he'd been upset, swearing off female company for months, but in the end he'd realised she'd been right—recognised what she'd seen in him when he'd taken off to work in a health post in the Himalayas a year later and again when he'd volunteered and been accepted as medical support to an Antarctic expedition for three months, not to mention the two months he'd spent in North-West China on a medical team.

'So, do you run off to the wilderness regularly?' the blonde asked, when he'd put some of these thoughts into words—answering some trite question about why a handsome man like him was still unattached.

'Not as often these days,' he admitted. 'Maybe I'm getting too old—too fond of my home comforts.'

She protested at that, said he couldn't possibly be that old, but he was remembering the restlessness he used to feel inside himself—the need to experience new things, to spend time out from his prescribed world every now and then. He'd always returned refreshed from his adventures, and with renewed enthusiasm for his job, pleased Kate had said no and not shackled him with a home and children, responsibilities he hadn't been ready to take on.

'So, where else would you like to go?' the woman asked, after ticking off the countries he'd mentioned on her fingers.

Across her shoulder he could see Anna approaching.

'Deepest, darkest Africa,' he heard his mouth say as his heart began to flutter arrhythmically in his chest and his lungs seized up completely.

'Wow, what an attractive woman!'

The blonde must have followed his gaze for she'd turned and repeated the accolade the kids had given Anna.

But 'wow' was hardly adequate. Anna moved across the room with the stately grace of a queen—if royalty were ever allowed to show so much skin. She was smiling at him, still a little tremulous, as if unable to believe that the beauty she'd seen in the mirror—and had to feel in the waves of admiration following her across the room—was really her.

'You look stunning,' he said, and meant it. Wondered if there were breath tests for intoxication of another kind, said yes when a waiter appeared with a drinks tray, downed the cool liquid in one gulp, then looked again.

The blonde had vanished—no doubt swallowed up by the floor—and Anna filled his vision. Most of the curls had been gathered up at the back of her head, but they'd also been treated in some way so they curled more tightly, especially the ones left loose around her face where their darker redness framed her pale ivory skin, giving her a luminous beauty he couldn't quite take in.

'What do you think?' she demanded as if she hadn't heard his initial reaction, couldn't read his shock in his face.

'It—it looks great,' he stammered, 'really great.' Wondered what the 'in' word was, what Josh might say. Perhaps that would get the message across.

Liz rescued him, all but skipping up to them, a broad smile proclaiming that her part in the proceedings had been successful.

'Anna, you look abso-bloody-lutely beautiful,' she announced. 'Boy, you sure knocked old bachelor Pete here for six. I saw his face as you walked across the room—that poor blonde had been doing quite well up till then, but after you appeared she might as well have been wallpaper.'

'It's only the hair,' Anna protested, pleased and more relaxed by Liz's comments. 'I'm not really beautiful—they just made me look that way.'

Whereupon she was pounced upon by someone else and whisked away for judging or presentation or something and Pete decided another glass of champagne might help clear his head.

Which it didn't. In fact, all it did was preclude him from driving home.

'I can drive as far as your place and take a cab home from there,' Anna told him a little later, sounding far too sober and practical for someone who looked like a Sex Goddess.

Hoped like hell he hadn't said that aloud. No, three glasses of champagne might affect his ability to drive, but not his brain.

'No, I won't allow that. We'll take a cab, I'll drop you off, then go on in it.'

He took her elbow, wanting to get her out of the place before any more male so-called hair-stylists came over to look at her 'hair'!

'That's ridiculous. It means you having to get back here tomorrow to collect your car. I've had one glass of champagne, and that was hours and hours ago. I'll drive. Or don't you trust me?'

'To drive?' he asked, thinking of all the ways he didn't trust her. Or trust himself with her.

'Of course. What else?' she demanded.

Couldn't answer—shrugged.

'Look, if you don't like the idea of my getting a cab from your place, why not let me drive us both to my place? You can stay the night—we've heaps of space and I even keep new toothbrushes for when the kids have friends staying unexpectedly. That way you'll get a good night's sleep and you'll have your car and can head home whenever you like in the morning.'

Good night's sleep with her under the same roof? It seemed unlikely but he couldn't come up with a valid objection.

Couldn't think of a reason to not kiss her either when she stopped his car in her driveway—switching off the lights so he didn't need to be embarrassed by the battered door, then turning towards him to thank him for a delightful evening.

'It was my pleasure,' he murmured, speaking softly so he'd have to get closer or she wouldn't hear. And once he was close enough it seemed a natural extension of the words to brush his lips across hers—as easy as breathing.

Or was as easy as breathing usually was when her faint skin-smell wasn't affecting his autonomic nervous system and shutting things down—or speeding them up. General upheaval within, whichever way you considered it.

He felt a little quiver in her lips so put a hand on her shoulder to hold her steady— warm flesh beneath his fingers—deepened the kiss, searching for her tongue, certain he had to do this—though why he didn't know.

'You'd make the Pope forget his vows,' he muttered, pulling away from her, struggling for breath, wondering what the hell was going on here.

'Are your vows so sacrosanct?' she asked.

When he didn't answer—couldn't really, given how he was feeling—she heard the silence as a no and added, 'Why? Was your parents' marriage unhappy? Do you think you'd be stifled within a permanent relationship? Isn't there room for compromise in most relationships? Is freedom from ties so very important to you?'

He wasn't sure why she was asking—which didn't matter as, apart from the one about his parents' marriage, which had been happy, he couldn't answer any of her questions.

'I'd better go,' he grumbled, hating the feeling of inadequacy that kept swamping him.

'You're staying here,' she reminded him, reaching out so her hand cupped his chin. and turning his head so he had to look into her eyes. 'Thanks again, it was a wonderful evening.'

Then she climbed out of the car, revealing the same seductive length of stockinged leg, led the way into the house, asked if he wanted anything to eat or drink and, when he'd refused all offers—that she'd made, anyway—showed him to a bedroom.

As he stripped off and slipped, naked, between the sheets he wondered what she wore to bed, then heard the kids' voices, asking questions, high-pitched ribaldry as they teased her about her hair, and realised she probably wore motherly cotton—or flannelette pyjamas, like he did.

But even in flannelette pyjamas her image disturbed his sleep and her perfume seemed to permeate the whole house, lingering in his nostrils, tantalising him when he moved in the comfortable bed.

Decided he should have taken that cab home.

He was certain of it when he awoke to the clattering sounds and last-minute instructions which usually accompanied an imminent departure.

A soft tap on the bedroom door, then a head appeared—this time surrounded with the more usual mass of softer curls.

'Sorry to desert you, but we're off to the lake for the day. There's food, tea, coffee and the morning paper in the kitchen. Help yourself, and just pull the front door shut when you leave.'

'You're going to the lake?'

He sat up quickly, remembered he was naked and pulled the sheet to his waist. She nodded and waited expectantly, but he couldn't think of anything else to say.

Well, he could think of plenty but it would all sound stupid. What about, How can you go the lake with Bill when you let me kiss you last night? Certainly couldn't say that!

Don't let him touch you. That was another possibility lingering in his head, but he could imagine her reaction to that one.

Wait, I'm coming with you. That might work, but could he bear to see her with Bill—close to Bill, smiling at his weak jokes, holding onto his waist when she rode behind him on the jet-ski?

'Have a nice time,' he said feebly, and waved. As the door shut, he lay back down on the bed, pulled the sheet over his head and wondered how he'd made such a monumental mess of his life.

An hour later, in suit pants and smoke-tainted business shirt, with the sleeves rolled up to look casual, he was surveying the other monumental mess he'd made—this time of her garage door.

Not the kind of damage you could bash out with a hammer.

Riddled with guilt, he phoned another cousin, Liz's brother who did carpentry and handyman work, and asked him to come and have a look. Which was why he was still at the Cranes' house six hours later, a new roller-shutter door hung and a remote control mechanism installed by way of apology.

'A bit of overkill, don't you think, mate?' Bill asked as Anna and the children played with the remote, making the door go up and down, demonstrating to each other how the sensor stopped it closing on either human beings or cars.

Pete shrugged. Bill might be uncomfortable about his being there, but both Josh and Jackie had echoed Anna's invitation to have a cool drink with them—perhaps stay for a light dinner.

'You could play Trivial Pursuit with us, be on the girls' side against Josh and Bill,' Jackie suggested. 'Josh reads the cards all the time and knows most of the answers so you'd be a big help.'

Pete glanced at Anna, but she was struggling with Josh over the control, winning in the end and closing the door for the last time. Did she really want him to stay or had politeness made her ask?

He glanced at Bill and knew exactly what he thought of the idea.

Opted to go, making excuses about phone calls to his family, letters to write, a good TV programme.

'Anna always tells us to offer only one excuse,' Jackie told him. 'She says offering more than one makes it sound as if you're making up reasons not to do whatever it is—makes you sound desperate.'

Pete ground his teeth. Bill was welcome to this family of know-alls. Said a gruff goodbye and walked out to the car, heard Anna call to him but didn't look back, waited until he was driving off before glancing their way—then waving casually.

One excuse, indeed!

Spent another week avoiding her, except at a hospital staff meeting where he introduced her to every unmarried male on the medical staff, thinking there might be safety for her in numbers.

Safety from what?

From the things he feared—like commitment, being tied down?

Perhaps she didn't want to be tied down, he decided, seeing her converse in the most polite and least flirtatious possible way with all the men. Josh may not realise it, but she might be counting off the days until he and Jackie left home so she could go off and do her own thing—as he had in the past.

Only he wasn't going to think about that 'in the past' bit right now. He was having sufficient trouble with the present.

When he looked again she was gone and he panicked—though he wasn't going to question that either.

Walked out of the big boardroom and down the passageway, asking people if they'd seen her—was she in the rest-rooms?

Heard a noise at the top of the fire stairs and opened the door to find her leaning against the wall on the top landing, tears streaming down her face.

It was only natural to take her in his arms, to hold her close and soothe her, mop away the tears, comfort and caress her—so distressed by her distress that his chest was hurting.

'Want to talk about it?' he asked, when her body had stopped shaking and her breathing had steadied.

She snorted and shook her head, then pushed herself away, wiping her fingers across her cheeks.

'Sorry! I didn't think anyone would notice my departure. I met up with Ryan Wallace. He was Ted's oncologist in the city—he's visiting up here this week. He didn't know I'd started working again—we'd lost touch. When the family, all of us, shifted back up here, we knew no treatment was going to help Ted, but Ryan tried to keep him pain-free—as you know, a near impossible task once cancer is in the bones. Seeing Ryan was a shock. It brought it all back—those last terrible few months— the pain he suffered—my guilt.'

She wasn't crying but she sounded like someone in need of a hug so he took her in his arms again.

'Your guilt? From what I've heard, you were marvellous. You did everything you could,' Pete scolded.

She rested her head on his chest and shook it, then lifted her hands to his shoulders and pressed herself against his body, as if trying to climb inside him to escape some terrible memory.

'Except kill him,' she said bleakly. 'I knew damn well it's what he wanted—that it was the only way I could have saved him such agonising suffering—but I'd see the kids sitting by his bed, still so young, and I'd tell myself a miracle might happen—that I couldn't take him away from them just yet. And I didn't do it.'

'We're trained to save lives not take them,' Pete whispered into the soft curls. 'He was a doctor, Anna, and he'd have known the prognosis as well as you did. Known he was dying and just how hard that death would be. Don't you think he could have got hold of morphine in the early stages—when he was first diagnosed—before he was too ill to work? If he'd wanted an easier path, he could have taken it, Anna. It was his responsibility, not yours.'

He felt the change in her, the tension easing from her body, her flesh softening, growing warm against his as hormonal urges swept away the last remnants of grief and sparked responses deep within his abdomen.

Kissed her with passion this time, deeply and determinedly, trying to wipe away not only the pain from her body but also Ted Crane from her physical memory.

She responded at first, escalating his desire, then once again struggled free, pushing him back against the wall. Looked into his eyes for a moment, then headed determinedly down the stairs.

'You're four floors up,' he called after her, furious at her desertion and at himself for kissing her like that at such a time.

Heard nothing but her footsteps, getting fainter and fainter, as she wound her way down the steps.

Avoidance was the only way. He'd go back to that—and good luck to Bill or Ken or anyone else who turned up in her path. The sooner she was married off, the better. Maybe then he could get on with his own life, make plans, talk to someone about working on an island somewhere in the Pacific next time he took extended leave. Hadn't that been another dream?

CHAPTER EIGHT

NOT that avoidance worked. Hard to avoid someone when you work with them twelve hours a day. But Pete did manage to introduce Anna to another couple of single men on the ancillary staff and Alex, another engineer friend from his university days.

Then, his duty to Josh—and possibly himself—done, he wrote off to various government and charitable organisations, enquiring about their need for a doctor in remote parts, and accepted David's invitation to help flush out a method for monitoring the new well-staff health scheme. Keeping busy had always been his way of distracting himself from other issues.

'First meeting Thursday after work in the Outpatients staff lounge,' David told him as they walked out of the building together early the following week.

What David didn't add was that he'd asked Anna to join them, so Pete found himself sitting beside her on the lounge. He noticed the shadows beneath her eyes and faint lines of tiredness in her cheeks.

Yet she gave no hint of weariness when she put forth her views, arguing for or against ideas others offered. After three hours they had the basis for a programme which would offer staff a range of times they could see doctors, therapists or dietitians, plus an idea for a series of lectures on general health issues—on why prevention was better than cure. Someone offered to institute a quit smoking programme and a paediatrician with an interest in psychology offered to run an effective parenting course.

'Perhaps we could take all this a step further—invite the general public to attend the courses and lectures,' David suggested, as the enthusiasm within the room began to grow. 'The hospital could become the focus of health promotion in the community rather than somewhere to go when you're sick.'

'That's how things should always have been,' someone agreed. 'And to a certain extent we do it. O and G run the women's health clinic, which gives occasional lectures to high school students about safe sex, and the dietitians have run healthy cooking courses from time to time. The problem is we've never integrated it.'

Pete felt the buzz in the room and knew that something different had begun—perhaps something as challenging as a few months' work in some far-flung country. The scheme would need co-ordination, and the enthusiasm would have to be fed with new ideas and suggestions if it wasn't to fizzle out.

'Do you think people will respond?' Anna asked him as they left the room, the excitement she'd displayed inside fading slightly as doubts overtook her.

'If we promote it properly, they will,' he assured her. 'It was a great idea to begin with our own hospital population and their families. I know it's spreading but that should still be the basis. And it's wonderful to see so many people in the hospital working together towards a common goal.' He grinned at her. 'Most of the time we're fighting each other for more staff or more funds—not conducive to a happy work atmosphere at all. Your theory behind it is right—so much of the illness we see in our work could have been prevented if the patient had been treated earlier. And not only is prevention better than treatment—it's cheaper.'

She smiled at him, but her eyes didn't crinkle at the corners and he knew it had been a half-hearted effort. Felt concern for her twisting in his gut.

'You look tired. Your two will have eaten by now so how about we stop somewhere that's on your way home and I buy you dinner? That'll save you having to feed yourself when you get back to the house.'

She looked up at him quickly, as if the offer had startled her.

'I don't think so,' she said, and the smile became more real, making her lips curl up at the corners and the dimple appear in her cheek.

'Got another date?' he asked—well, it may have been more of a demand. He was aggravated enough to demand.

She pretended to look shocked.

'On a weeknight? No way!'

But he found it hard to accept—both her refusal and the lack of an excuse—and the aggravation followed him through to the next day.

'Teenager with severe abdominal pain coming in,' Margie called to him. 'Anna's in the lounge, talking to someone about the health scheme. Will you take it?'

He glanced around their waiting room. One patient holding a pad to a scalp wound, which Wendy said would only need a dressing, and that was it—a quiet moment in the day.

Walked beside the gurney into the trauma room, introducing himself to the patient who was pale and sweating profusely, her legs drawn up to her belly as if to guard her pain.

'Are you Mrs Affleck?' he asked the woman accompanying the girl.

She smiled at him and shook her head.

'I'm a teacher at her school. We've notified Gillian's mother—she should be here shortly.'

Which made the patient look even sicker.

Kim was with him, already attaching leads for an ECG. Wendy arrived and took up position on the other side of the table, wrapping a blood pressure cuff around the patient's arm. Pete talked, asking questions, explaining he wanted to feel her abdomen, enquiring about her menstrual cycle, about sexual activity.

His patient looked shocked, denied any such thing, but the presentation suggested more a gynaecological problem than appendicitis, particularly with uterine bleeding which she assured him was her regular menses.

Her blood pressure was way too low, suggesting blood loss somewhere, and he stopped questioning to take blood for typing and investigation and to start fluids running into her. At which stage, Mrs Affleck arrived.

With Anna right behind her.

'Social mother,' he heard Anna whisper to him, while Mrs Affleck ordered him to fix her daughter immediately.

'Pain relief, that's what she needs. Poor darling, she's like me, always suffers terribly—every month—it's agony. I give her codeine and sometimes just a little gin—my mother always recommended gin.'

Pete felt his eyes rolling in his head, then a finger prod his back.

'Get Mrs Affleck and the teacher out of here,' Anna hissed at him. 'I want to talk to Gillian.'

What was he, a miracle-worker?

He tried the mother first.

'Could I speak to you outside for a moment?' Wondered what the hell he could say to her if she agreed.

She did agree, but not immediately, turning to the teacher first and thanking her for her concern, the words an unmistakable dismissal.

The three of them left the trauma room together and Pete waited until the teacher had departed, before repeating the questions he'd asked Gillian—about the youngster's cycle, her social life, sexual activity.

'Of course she's not sexually active,' Mrs Affleck declared, obviously affronted by the thought that her fourteen-year-old daughter could know anything of such behaviour. She then turned the attack back on him. 'What about appendicitis? Have you thought of that? Are you a specialist or just an intern of some kind? What are your qualifications for treating my daughter?'

He hoped Anna was achieving something while he held the mother at bay, reeling off his qualifications—among the best in emergency medicine in the state—and explaining why it wasn't likely to be appendicitis. Then Ken Riddell appeared and Pete knew Anna had gleaned some additional information from the girl. Felt guiltily glad it was Ken, not he, who would be ruining Mrs Affleck's day with a discussion of her daughter's 'non-existent' sex life.

Only it wasn't Ken who explained to the woman, and comforted her as Gillian was prepared for transfer upstairs where an emergency operation would be necessary to remove the ectopic pregnancy which had ruptured her Fallopian tube and was probably causing peritonitis even as they treated her.

It was Anna, seemingly always there when she was needed, listening without judgement, although Pete guessed she was silently blaming the mother for much of what had happened. He'd seen it before when she'd stood by the Wilsons after Naomi had been admitted and had come away from the ward seething at their lack of understanding.

He waited until she returned from escorting the patient upstairs—Gillian's hand in Anna's, not her mother's—then spoke to her about it.

'Did Gillian talk to you because you're a woman, do you think?' he asked, thinking if that were so he should try to recruit more women to the department so patients could have a choice of male or female.

She smiled at the question, considered it for a moment, then replied. 'I cannot tell a lie—I had inside information. She's at school with Jackie and I knew she was serious about this boy in the year above them.' She sighed and looked seriously worried.

'I don't think there's anything you can do to stop kids these days becoming sexually involved, but I hate to think of girls as young as Gillian being sexually active. I'm always afraid they're doing it for the wrong reason—for popularity—but, then, who the hell am I to be handing out advice on sex?'

Her shoulders lifted in a shrug and she turned as if about to walk away, but he couldn't let it pass—had to ask.

'Why? Were you a late starter?'

Then was sorry he'd asked because her cheeks flushed, and the worried look became one of embarrassment.

'Hey, don't answer that—it was a presumptuous question!' he said quickly.

The flush subsided slightly, but she remained where she was, watching him. Assessing him?

'You could say that,' she muttered after what seemed like minutes. Then she grinned. 'In fact, I haven't started yet. That's what makes it so damned hard to talk to the kids. What on earth would a thirty-year-old virgin know?'

Whirled around and this time she did leave the room, but he followed her, caught her arm and turned her towards him, making her step back inside the office so they were out of public view.

'You've been married twice and you're still a virgin?' he demanded, wanting to laugh but knowing it wasn't really a laughing matter. It was something she was seriously concerned about if the look in her eyes was any guide. 'Going for annulments each time, were you?'

She shook off his hand and walked across to sit down at her desk.

'You can laugh,' she said, guessing his reaction. 'In fact, I laugh about it myself when

I'm feeling on top of things. But it's no laughing matter when it comes to, well, reality. How can I talk to the kids about sex?' She looked away from him.

'Talk to myself?' she added more softly.

He guessed it was something she wanted—perhaps needed—to discuss, and felt a surge of pleasure that she'd chosen him.

'Why?' he asked, then wondered if she'd realise what he was asking.

'My first husband was a friend I made at university. He was from an island nation in the Pacific and there'd been a lot of unrest there. It turned out he'd only been on a visitor's visa while he'd studied in Australia and when he'd finished he'd stayed on. He was about to be deported so I married him.'

'To stop the deportation?' He was pleased she'd guessed which 'why'! Pleased by the story, but in a different way.

'For that reason alone. Later we arranged an annulment, and when the political unrest was sorted out he was free to go home. In fact, he's a government minister over there now.'

'And Ted?'

She smiled as if remembering—love softening her eyes, making her mouth tilt just a little at the corners.

'Ted and Sylvia Crane were my salvation,' she said quietly. 'I was a kid as wild as Naomi Wilson, although without the stability of her parents. My mother… Something happened…'

Her eyes glazed as she pulled a curtain across that memory and he remembered her talking about angst. Wanted to ask and knew it wasn't the moment, knew there were other things she *would* tell now. Waited while she regathered her composure, spoke again.

'I was fostered out and misbehaved enough for no one to want me on a permanent basis. I like the excuse of attention-seeking, but I think I was probably just plain bad at that stage. My last foster-family lived near the Cranes and I used to babysit for them—which shows just how great they were to trust a hell-raiser like me with their infants.'

'They must have seen something good in you in spite of all your efforts to be bad to the bone!' he teased, and her smile broadened.

'Maybe,' she admitted. 'Anyway, it was Ted who discovered I had quite a useful brain beneath all the rebellion, and convinced me to use it. I went through my last two years at high school as an A student and followed my idol into medicine. In the end, I married Ted for love, but it was a different kind of love. I wanted to give something back to him, to Sylvia as well, really, and to Jackie and Josh, who'd been a big part of my life for a long time.'

And she missed him—was still hurting from his death. He could hear it in her voice and see it in the bleakness in her eyes. He wanted to hold her, comfort her, cherish her a little, but knew he couldn't—that holding her was too seductive, and cherishing disastrous.

'I'd be happy to talk to Josh, or have him know he can come to me if ever he wants to talk man stuff,' he found himself saying. 'And, technically, you must know enough to talk to Jackie.'

She nodded, then he heard her chuckle.

'I can talk to both the kids about sex,' she admitted, 'although I don't bring personal experience into it.' She looked at him, hesitated, turned away, and he guessed it was for herself she needed counselling. Felt anger surge as he wondered which of the chaps she was seeing was putting pressure on her, decided he didn't want to know and was relieved when he was called to see a patient.

The aftermath of that strange conversation was a distance between them—well, she seemed to have distanced herself from him, doing more of the avoiding than he was. He told himself this was good—it was what he wanted—but doubts and aggravation seethed beneath his skin, and the attraction he felt for her was exacerbated rather than cooled by her detachment.

'Policeman to see you,' Margie announced a few days later when the normal rush of the early morning had subsided and he was catching up on some paperwork. 'It's about the Wilson girl.'

His first thought was that the parents had made a complaint about him treating her without consent, but he soon realised he was wrong.

'She'd broken into the house she was leaving through a partially open window. The owners of the place are pressing charges,' the policeman, who introduced himself as Colin Wright, explained. 'We need to speak to who-ever it was who removed the jewellery from the lass's pocket, make sure he or she is will-ing to testify.'

He remembered seeing the sparkly stuff in Anna's hand, but had she pulled it from the pocket of the girl's torn and bloodied uniform? He buzzed the desk, asked Margie to send Anna in if she wasn't busy. These days she was doing her paperwork in the lounge rather than in the office, and he suspected that's where she'd been for she dropped a folder on the second desk, before shaking hands with the policeman.

'I pulled them out of her pocket but I don't like the idea of testifying against the child,' she said bluntly. Glanced at Pete as if unsure how he'd react to what was coming, then added in a firm voice, 'At the moment, I'm one of the few adult friends that kid has.'

No wonder she looked guilty! And tired. Did she never stop?

'I visited her in the ward here a couple of times, then her parents transferred her to the private hospital and...'

'And?' Pete prompted, wanting to hear just how far this latest good samaritan act had gone.

'I called in there as well—in fact, I still do whenever I have time. Her parents visit after work—a ten minute duty call at about six-thirty each evening—so I go before or after that and Jackie and Josh both go at weekends.'

She sounded defiant and he knew exactly why. Forgot the policeman as he pointed it out.

'You already work long hours here, which takes a toll of you both physically and emotionally. A good emergency doctor can't afford to get caught up in every case that comes through the door. You'll burn out—I've told you that.'

She didn't look at all abashed—in fact, she met his eyes and tilted her chin as if she was spoiling for a fight.

'I don't get involved with every case,' she argued. 'Naomi was—is—different.' She turned to the policeman. 'I don't think charging her will help,' she said, then added honestly, 'although I have no psychology training so it's a feeling, not a medical opinion. The child needs love, not a court case. She needs a few people in the world who believe she's a worthwhile human being. Dragging her to court is going to diminish her in her own eyes—reinforce all the negative stuff she already believes about herself.'

She darted a glance at Pete and he guessed that whatever was coming next was going to make him angrier.

'Could I talk to the people who are making the charges, perhaps persuade them to take some other measures?'

The policeman looked doubtful.

'She'd only appear in the children's court,' he said uncertainly. 'Very low key and there's restricted access to the records afterwards.'

But Pete saw Anna shudder, knew she was speaking from the heart—and possibly experience—found himself backing her up.

'Could we try speaking to the people?'

Again the policeman looked dubious, then he shrugged and shook his head.

'Actually, we might have soothed things over with them in the early stages if the parents hadn't intervened,' he admitted. 'Seems they approached the complainants with an offer of money—restitution, they said—but the victims saw it as a bribe and got their dander up. Reckon kids should face up to their guilt, not have their parents buy them out of trouble.'

Pete heard Anna sigh, but he suspected it didn't signify capitulation—merely a strategic retreat while she replotted her attack.

'I do agree with that,' she told Colin, 'but could we do the guilt trip some other way? Isn't there some programme now of having the perpetrators meeting with their victims? Couldn't we try it that way—perhaps have Naomi work for these people by way of restitution or punishment?'

'I doubt the Wilsons would go along with that,' Colin told her. 'Now their bribery attempt has failed they want the business over and done with. They know her name will be suppressed in a children's court and the proceedings kept out of newspapers—'

'So *they're* OK!' Anna said bitterly. 'They don't give a damn about their daughter or the effect such an ordeal will have on her.' She paused, her eyes on the policeman. 'Couldn't we attempt it through confrontation if you advocated it—couldn't you tell the parents the victims like that idea better?'

He smiled at her, and Pete knew the man was weakening. Wouldn't anyone, with those blue eyes pleading for the cause?

'That's after I've convinced the victims that they do like that idea better,' he said.

Got a beaming smile from Anna in reply.

'Well, I'm willing to help with that,' she assured him, 'and I'd also be happy to tell Naomi about it and go with her, see that she carries out whatever punishment is meted out.'

Colin stood up, shook Pete's hand, shook his head at Anna and said, 'I'll see what I can do first. I'll be in touch.'

Pete waited until he was well away, before turning on his assistant.

'She's not your child—you can't take over her life!' Realised he was yelling as the words bounced back off the walls at him. Not that it seemed to affect Anna, who had that stubborn chin tilted again and a mulish set to her lovely lips.

'I know she's not my child and I have no intention of taking over her life, but she and Jackie were quite friendly once, according to Jackie, although Naomi's younger, and I see no reason why that friendship shouldn't continue.'

'And Josh? Where does he fit in? Visiting her in hospital, indeed!'

'He's a mentor in his high school—like a junior counsellor—someone the younger kids can go to if they need advice or support. He drives Jackie up to visit Naomi, and why wait outside if she enjoys the extra company?'

'She'll probably fall in love with him,' he warned when he could think of no other objection but knew he had to argue.

'That won't be the worst thing that ever happens to her,' Anna pointed out. 'When I was only a little older than her, I was madly in love with Ted Crane.' She smiled as if remembering that puppy love. 'Ted and Sylvia were both very gentle with me, and Josh has their genes—he'll handle it without hurting Naomi.'

Was he stymied in this argument? Thought so—until he remembered his prime objection.

'I'm still against you taking on too much patient contact out of work hours. You're already carrying a big load as a working mother, and to add patient visits and the emotional stress of shouldering other people's problems—it's too much.'

'And you didn't visit Janice Jennings last weekend?' she countered. 'Didn't go up to the ward the day her mother was transferred from ICU to check she wasn't having trouble with either her father or Tim?'

He straightened in his chair.

'I was in the ward on other business,' he said stiffly, then he scowled at her. 'But I had been worried about that bikie fellow, about you matching them up like that—interfering in their lives.'

She raised both eyebrows this time and he saw the glint of anger in her eyes.

'I did not match them up,' she retorted. 'They did that themselves—met and clicked, nothing more. I had nothing to do with Tim moving into her house, but if we're talking about matching people up, well, you've brought up something I've been wanting to say to you but up till now haven't because I didn't want to upset you—or I wasn't angry enough.'

She took a deep breath and began again, glaring at him in case he hadn't already caught on to the fact that she was seriously annoyed with him.

'I don't know why you're doing it but I want you to stop casting single men in my path. Every time I turn around, you're introducing me to someone else. I'm very happy with my life, thank you very much, and if you're worried about my physical well-being, how do you think I can handle the working hours here and a social life as well? So stop it, do you hear?'

He heard all right—in fact, most of the floor must have heard. Didn't like her being angry with him so he blamed Josh.

'He asked me to,' he bleated, not unduly concerned about getting out of trouble by betraying a fellow male. 'He and Jackie are both anxious to see you—' Mentally deleted 'married off' and substituted, 'Happy! They're worried about you being all alone when they leave home, and they think you're such a good mother you should have children of your own.'

There, that's telling her! Glanced her way to see how she was taking it and was surprised to see a single tear bead slowly on her eyelashes, then overflow, sliding down her cheek.

'Those silly brats,' she said in a choky kind of voice, smiling at him and blinking watery eyes. 'Fancy thinking like that! Fancy them worrying about me.'

Somehow this conversation wasn't going the way he'd thought it would.

'Well,' he demanded, 'aren't you going to do something about it? Don't you see their point?'

She pulled a handkerchief from her pocket and blew her nose, then bunched the scrap of material in her fingers and studied it for a while.

'Well?' he repeated, needing, for some reason, to hear her answer.

'I don't think so,' she said sadly. 'And I mean it when I say no more men, Pete.'

But she didn't look up so he couldn't read her face, see her eyes.

'Why not?' he persisted. 'Are you determined to die a virgin? Perhaps you should go the whole way—join a nunnery, devote your life to good works, cut yourself off from normal social contacts, live vicariously through your children and the lame ducks you adopt with such alacrity. Is that all you want? Will that be enough for you? Do you just look like a real flesh and blood, sensuous bloody woman when inside you're nothing but a robot?'

Now she looked up—and seemed startled. But that was OK—so was he. In fact, he'd been shocked by the rage he'd felt, and heard it reflected in his voice.

'No, that's not it at all,' she said bluntly. 'And, yes, I am real flesh and blood, Peter Jackson. But it just so happens that the flesh and blood part has already fallen in love with someone else—someone unattainable—and I'm damned if I'm going to offer a second-best love to any other man so just stop throwing them at my head and keep out of my private life!'

She stormed from the room, leaving him stunned—and in the grip of such pain he wondered if he were having a heart attack.

Well, he'd poked his nose in where it didn't belong—and got it bitten off! He'd asked and now he knew.

Unattainable?

What the hell did that mean?

Oh, no! She'd fallen for some married guy!

Thought back, reasonably certain she'd been heart-whole when she'd arrived to work with him—she'd certainly seemed interested in meeting the first few men he'd produced. She'd even gone out with them.

So it was after she'd arrived here, and if he discounted patients he was left with staff. Which male staff did she see regularly?

Orderlies—well, they were all either too young or too old as far as he could figure— and David Johnson in Outpatients.

Damn, and he'd introduced them at his dinner party! Anna had known from the start— the first meeting—that he was married. Maybe she fell in love with married men as a kind of defence reflex. Things couldn't get out of control if the object of worship was unattainable.

None of which made him feel any better.

Had David encouraged her in any way?

The thought brought the rage roaring back through his blood and he had to breathe deeply, tell himself it was nothing to do with him, remind himself that it was none of his business.

Wondered what the staff would think if he went home sick!

CHAPTER NINE

PETE managed to get through the day, but over the ensuing days, seeing Anna working with David on the well-staff proposal made him wonder if deepest, darkest Africa might not be a good idea. Tried to analyse why it bothered him when it was none of his business— watched her carefully and realised that she'd never betray her feelings to David or anyone else. So his friend's marriage was safe. He should be thankful, not concerned.

He was thinking about marriage in general—not David's in particular—as he left work the following Friday. A familiar figure with a tangle of dreadlocks was hovering outside the door.

'Hey, Josh! How are things? You waiting for Anna? I thought she'd left earlier.'

The lad shrugged his footballer's shoulders and managed to look about six in spite of his height and bulk.

'She knows I'm here,' he said defensively, then he looked up at Pete. 'I wanted to ask you if we could have a talk some time, you know, about chicks and stuff like that. I mean, Anna's good, like, but I don't—well, she—it's different for her, being a woman and all.'

The words rushed out as if released by a pressure valve.

'Now?' Pete asked, and saw Josh's surprise.

'Gee, no, not now. Friday night, like, you'll have a date. I don't want to be a nuisance—Anna said don't be a nuisance when she told me what you said about talking to me if I wanted.'

Pete hid a smile and wondered how many seventeen-year-olds took enough notice of their mothers—or stepmothers—to be able to repeat their words.

'Now's not bad.' he told Josh. 'I was going to order a pizza on the way home, then eat it in front of the TV, washing it down with a can of beer. You're under age for the beer, but I'm sure there's soft drink in the fridge.'

'Really? You mean it? Now, as in tonight?'

His eagerness made Pete feel old—how long since he'd felt such a surge of enthusiasm?

'Now, as in tonight,' he assured Josh. 'Let's go to the car and you can use my mobile to call Anna and tell her where you are. Have you got wheels?'

'No, my car's off the road at the moment— waiting for a new water pump.' Josh loped along beside him, reminding him of a large and amiable puppy.

'If you like, you can stay the night and I'll drop you home in the morning.'

'Oh, no, I can jog home from your place. Anna showed us where you live—it's not that far across town and I need the exercise.'

Now Pete felt tired as well as unenthusiastic.

'Not at night, you won't jog home,' he argued. 'Anna would never forgive me if I let something happen to you.'

Josh agreed to stay, made the phone call, made another to order pizza, then asked technical questions about the Land Cruiser all the way home. Pete found himself battling for answers, although he prided himself on knowing his vehicle and its capabilities.

'You interested in cars?' he asked Josh as they pulled into his drive.

The teenager grinned at him.

'Not really—well, I know enough to keep mine running, I guess—but I thought it might be a good thing to talk about for a while, you know!'

Pete did know, and he smiled, surprised by the ingenuous admission. He took the lad inside, found him a drink, then threw the television guide at him.

'Find something we can half watch while we talk,' he suggested, knowing from experience that 'talks' didn't always flow quite as easily as the mental rehearsals.

But this talk was different.

'Heavens, did you think I wanted to talk about, like, sex?' Josh had exploded into laughter when Pete made a tentative foray into this field. 'No, man, it's about life that I'm confused.'

Well, good for you! Pete thought grumpily. Glad you've got the sex thing sorted out. Might make it easier for you in your thirties.

Then realised what Josh had said.

'Life? It's not the world's most easily encapsulated subject. Was there some specific section of it? Could we narrow it down?'

Josh laughed again, obviously far more at ease in this situation than Pete was.

Then bit by bit he explained his doubts.

'Relationships confuse the best of us, mate,' Pete counselled him—and meant it!

'But not you,' Josh protested. 'You've worked out what you want. You must have known from early on. I mean, how will I know when I'm eighteen if a particular girl I'm attracted to is going to be the kind I have a fling with, or a serious relationship with, or if maybe she's marriage material. How do I tell?'

Good question! Unanswerable question! And Josh thought *he* could help?

Pete considered it carefully, knowing whatever he said wouldn't take the place of experience but not wanting to short-change the boy with facile platitudes or jokey remarks.

'I don't think you ever know in the beginning,' he began, while his head told him that was wrong. He'd known the minute he'd set eyes on her—well, the second time, you had to discount the interview—that there was something special about Anna. 'That's why I'd always advise anyone to take things slowly. Give yourself a chance to get to know each other before you get too physically involved. Then wait and see what happens.

'Relationships are like footballers. You know, you get some guys come on the team and they play really well for a season and everyone touts them as a rising star, then they fizzle out—never do much, don't train or put commitment into it—and disappear.'

Josh nodded but didn't seem much the wiser. Nor would I be, Pete decided, and tried again.

'Perhaps they're more like the game than the people in it. You know how you go into different sports when you're a kid—martial arts, soccer, tennis—trying them all out? Then you find one you really enjoy and that's worth sticking to, and you put all your effort into that. When you're young you meet girls, fancy perhaps one in particular, take her out. It could happen that she turns out to be the for-ever-after one for you—it happened that way with one of my brothers. He's married to his first girlfriend. Or you might realise it's not right for you…or for her…' He came to a halt. 'How am I doing? This is new to me, this talking about relationships stuff.'

Josh grinned at him.

'I'm getting the drift,' he said. 'Was that how it was with you? Did you not find the sport you wanted to play badly enough to commit all your energy to it?'

Tricky question! He hesitated, then tried to reply honestly, working his way through his feelings as he formed the words.

'I've always believed I made a conscious decision not to get too involved because I didn't want to play team sports— if it's not too corny to go back to that analogy. I wanted to do so many things, go places families couldn't go, and I believed it wouldn't be fair on a partner or hypothetical children. Now I'm not too sure. Maybe I could have managed to still do what I wanted within the parameters of a marriage, or maybe you're right—the person for whom I'd have given it all up just never came along.'

'So, are you lonely now? Do you regret that decision? You're not that old—surely you could still find someone if you wanted to settle down.'

Pete felt the weight of his years press on his shoulders, wondered if he looked as if he were dwindling into senility and chuckled at Josh's image of him.

'If my aging heart could stand the strain of courtship, I probably could,' he joked, then realised Josh had taken it seriously—was looking concerned. He steered the conversation away from his heart, although the joke was less funny to him as well when he considered it later.

They talked sport now, pure sport, drifted back to speak of men and women, of kindness and consideration as important aspects of any relationship, of differences in women that men would never fathom.

'Just accept them as they are, and listen to them,' Pete advised. 'Growing up with sisters taught me that. You can't change them and usually you can't fix things for them—not emotional things—but if you listen they seem to be able to work it out themselves so that's my sole piece of advice, which, I should admit, I rarely follow myself. I tend to forget it when faced with an upset woman and want to put things right my way.'

'They do get upset easily,' Josh agreed. 'Well, Jackie does. Anna never seems to change. She gets a bit quieter and looks tired— that's the only indication we ever have that she's out of sorts.'

'She's been looking tired lately,' Pete said, and got a frowning glance from Josh.

'Yeah! I thought you might have known what was wrong. Maybe I shouldn't have got you to fix her up with those men. She was happy to be going back to work, but with a social life as well it might have been too much all at once.'

Pete bit his tongue, longing to ask which of the men she was seeing most regularly, wanting to know who was still around in Anna's life, knowing it was none of his business.

A police drama began on TV and Josh was soon absorbed in it, leaving Pete prey to the doubts and questions the strange conversation had raised.

He arrived at work on Monday to find Anna in front of his poster—right where she'd been the first morning she'd come to work. Wished he could start again in their relationship—personal, not professional.

'When do you begin raising money, Heart-throb?' she asked. 'How's this a fund-raising idea?'

His insides knotted and he strained his ears, hoping an approaching siren might stop this conversation before it started.

'It's the hospital fête next Saturday—you must have heard about it,' he said.

'I have,' she responded politely. 'I spent the weekend making jam. I know how bottled jam makes money—you sell it. Do they sell you as well, auction you to the highest bidder?'

He felt his cheeks heat, which was ridiculous—he hadn't blushed since adolescence.

'You'll see,' he muttered, and walked away, hoping to escape her by going to his office—remembered it was her office as well.

But he did escape for she didn't follow, taking the first patient of the morning instead. And his time in the office was limited as the usual trickle soon built to a steady flow.

'Get her into the trauma room,' he heard Anna yell when his stomach was telling him he should stop for lunch but the flow still hadn't eased.

He asked Wendy to finish dressing the man's leg ulcers and walked out of the cubicle to see Anna, guiding a gurney into the first trauma room.

'Susan Hepworth, her name is—she fainted in the chair,' she said to him, and he recalled his idle remark the day Anna had begun work. 'Febrile, admission notes show she's been feeling unwell—sore throat, diarrhoea.'

Pete grabbed the chart and read it, didn't see what he was looking for, called for Kim who'd taken the details.

'Was she menstruating? Did you ask?'

Kim shook her head, while Anna caught on quickly.

'Toxic shock? It would explain the fever and the rash. We haven't time to wait for confirmation from the lab—let's get her stabilised.'

Kim and Anna checked, found and removed a tampon, while he fitted an oxygen mask over the patient's mouth and nose, started IV fluid running into her veins.

'Get another port going in her other arm,' he told Anna. 'Take blood for Pathology first. Kim, blood pressure. Anna…'

Stopped to think. Had to monitor fluid status but catheterising her could carry the infection to her bladder. Control the infection later—it was already causing havoc in her body.

'A CVP monitor then a catheter to check her urine output—'

'I'll be careful,' Anna responded, and he knew she shared his concerns.

'Her systolic pressure's dropping.'

'Dopamine—we'll infuse it. What's her weight?'

Heard Kim's reply—a guess? He doubted it. She was a top admission nurse—not her fault she hadn't asked about the woman's cycle as it wasn't on the admission forms. Worked out the dosage and infusion rate and set it up on the drip. Now all he had to do was tackle the infection—take samples of her other body fluids for lab testing so they could use specific antibiotics later but get started now with a broad-spectrum staph-fighter.

'Are you going to keep her here until we get some lab results or send her upstairs?' Anna asked when they had their patient as comfortable as she could be with drips and tubes and catheters attached all over her body.

He hesitated. She was seriously ill, but was she bad enough for Intensive Care to take? He knew space was at a premium up there and doubted it, but he was wary about someone monitoring her status on a ward which had fewer nursing staff than he did down here.

'Keep her here,' he decided, 'for another hour at least to see if she's responding to the drugs. Kim, you stay with her.'

He followed Anna out of the room and into turmoil, with patients complaining about being kept waiting, another emergency coming through the door and ambulance sirens heralding more of the same.

Worked on, hearing Anna's quiet voice through the curtains as they assessed and processed patients like objects on a factory production line.

'I hate days like this when you can't give proper attention to patients as individuals,' Anna grumbled, when they met at the coffee-machine and took a few minutes' break to gulp down the restorative liquid.

'Learn to live with it,' he told her. 'As Huntley grows, we're going to have more and more days like this. With recent cuts in government funding, I'll be lucky to keep my two-doctor policy in place here. Once Admin starts whittling away at costs, anything could happen.'

'Then you'll have to work harder at the fête, won't you?' she advised, a teasing glint in her eyes. 'Raise more money to pay my salary.'

He shivered at the thought.

'I wish I could make jam,' he told her, then moved away before she could question him again.

Went back to the mêlée, thinking about the fête and his 'fund-raising', until Kim's cry for assistance brought him racing to the trauma room—Anna hot on his heels.

'Her heart's gone crazy,' Kim said, pounding her fist on the patient's chest in an effort to jolt it back to a normal rhythm.

'She's arrested,' Anna said quietly, and the ritual dance began, thick gel on the paddles, a jolt of electricity, intubate so they could keep oxygen flowing into her lungs, drugs to encourage the heart to work with the next shock. Feelings of despair and helplessness, not hope, although he was usually confident he could save his patients.

Three times, three shocks, the heart had given up, he could feel futility tugging at his skin—then Kim's cry.

'It's settled, look, the lines are regular.'

Now he *could* send her to Intensive Care, could justify his demand for her admittance to the specialist unit. Took her up himself, praying the fluid and drugs would now be allowed to work, that she was over the worst. Too young to die.

'I'm glad she responded. She was too young to die.' Anna repeated his reaction as they sat in the lounge later that evening, too tired to move, trying to gather enough energy to drive to their respective homes. 'I kept thinking of Jackie. It's something I warned her about a few years ago, using super-absorbent tampons, but I must remind her and persuade her to vary her use of them at all times. It happens so quickly. As Kim said, even when she came in she was only feeling unwell—a little dizzy, worried about the rash, about her fingers peeling.'

'I've only seen it once before, when I was a student,' Pete said, worrying about Jackie himself. 'I'll look up the incidence of it if ever I regain enough strength to open a book.'

Thought about the responsibility of having kids—the things you had to remember to tell them—worrying about what could happen if you forgot something. Responsibility! Something he'd managed to avoid in his personal life.

Heard Anna yawn and saw her eyelids drooping closed. With the red hair fanned around her head, her limbs and body relaxed, she looked like a discarded doll, the stuffing all gone from her.

Yet she had to drive home. So did he. Get moving or you'll go to sleep here!

'Do you think it would be easier to work together if we lived together—or would it be harder?' he asked, following a train of thought which had begun with driving home—perhaps if only one of them had to drive they might make it!

'Is this a hypothetical question?' she asked, her voice slightly strained—but that was probably tiredness.

'I think so,' he said, and explained.

'And which of us did you envisage doing the driving?' she asked languidly, lifting her feet and propping them on the coffee-table so she could lie further back in the chair. 'Not me, I hope. I'm knackered!'

'Now, there's a nice, ladylike expression,' he said, but she'd made him smile and he immediately felt slightly better. 'Come on, I'll drive. I'll take you home then collect you in the morning. I can't be any fairer than that, now, can I?'

She turned to look at him as if trying to figure out some ulterior motive. He saw the tiredness Josh had mentioned, and something else—deeper—unreadable. Sighed because she was a puzzle he couldn't fathom and she was occupying far too much of his thoughts.

Particularly with the David business. He'd watched her closely enough when they were together—and made sure he was with them whenever they met—but he'd seen no sign of any interest on her part, certainly no indication of a hidden passion.

But would one see a hidden passion? Surely the hidden part precluded that—

'What did you say?'

She smiled at him.

'I thought you'd nodded off. I said yes, actually. I accepted your kind offer to drive me home, but if you're going to go to sleep at the wheel perhaps I should drive you.'

'No, no, I was just thinking.'

He scrambled to his feet, pleased his thoughts weren't readable, waited while she retrieved her briefcase from the office, then walked her out to his car.

'Moon over the car park,' she remarked, looking up to where a huge yellow orb was dominating the eastern horizon. 'Think anyone will ever make a love song of it?'

He glanced towards her, saw the slight smile crinkling her eyes and making her lips curl and knew *he* could, knew anywhere where she was would be a love song.

Felt his chest tighten, his lungs crunch, decided he was having a heart attack. It had to be that—couldn't be anything else.

Definitely not love.

Not now—after all this time of believing it wasn't for him.

And definitely not with a woman who loved someone else!

'Are you OK? Look, how about we go in my car? I'll drive *you* home.'

He saw the anxiety clouding her eyes, the smile gone.

'I'm all right,' he assured her, lying through his teeth. 'Minor infarct—nothing to be concerned over.'

She slapped him on the shoulder—hard.

'Don't you ever, ever joke about something like that,' she stormed. 'Ever, you hear? Now, tell me, are you in pain? Do you have chest pains? Bloody doctors! They're the very worst when it comes to looking after themselves or taking notice of warning signs—and men are worse than women.'

She then burst into tears, completing the farce, didn't wait for him to answer her about pain but strode across to her car, got in, slammed the door and started the engine.

'Well, how's that for concern?' he muttered to himself, as she drove away. 'Here I could be having a heart attack in the car park and she's driving off and leaving me stranded.'

Well, hardly stranded. There were at least eight people walking slowly towards the hospital, their attention more on his little scene with Anna than their destination.

And he wasn't having a heart attack—this was a very different kind of pain. Incurable, most likely.

Made it home, and back the next day, got through it without too much contact, although his body had now begun to misbehave whenever she appeared, as if his mental acknowledgment of his interest in her had given it permission to cavort in a most unseemly fashion.

Hoped like hell it didn't show. It was one thing to go through the rest of his life as the victim of unrequited love, but quite another to appear foolish in the eyes of others over it.

'We've got that meeting with Naomi and her "victims" tomorrow night,' Anna said to him late in the day. 'Are you still happy to go along with this? She's out of hospital now, but I don't think the parents are being very supportive about it. I think they'd have been far happier paying a fine and forgetting it.'

'Are they coming?' he asked, channelling his frustration into anger against these people he didn't know—quite looking forward to a confrontation.

'No way,' Anna told him. 'It's only going ahead because Naomi herself said she'd like to meet them and apologise. Mrs Wilson has already delivered her opinion of me—not very flattering—and of interfering "do-gooders" in general.'

'Why do you get involved?' he asked, wanting to know but also wanting to keep her talking as he'd learned that being near her was better than not being near her. Which showed how sick he was!

'I suppose because no one did it for me—not until the Cranes came into my life. Most of my foster-parents were good, kind people, but they were stretched to their emotional limits, had no more to give—or not to me, anyway.'

'Won't you reach that stage?' he asked her. 'You've already got emotional responsibilities to Josh and Jackie—how far can you stretch?'

She smiled at him, and he saw a tinge of sadness in her eyes.

'Far enough,' she assured him, then she walked away.

He shook his head. The situation mystified him.

He could have sworn that sadness was directed at him—a slip on her part, but definitely connected with him.

But why would *he* be making her sad?

Because he didn't want her overreaching herself, burning out?

No, she was more likely to be angry over that.

He recalled what he'd said to Josh about women liking someone to listen to them. He'd get her to talk. No good here—they were always too busy. What if…?

'How about we grab a bite to eat after we've done our thing with Naomi tomorrow night?' he suggested later, trying to make it sound extremely casual although in his mind he was thinking candlelight and violins and roses on the table.

'That might be fun,' she agreed with about as much enthusiasm as if he'd offered her an enema.

But he wasn't going to put off by a lack of joy on her part and he whistled through the rest of that day and the next, buoyed by the thought of the treat ahead of him.

Not that things worked out that way. The 'victims', Mr and Mrs Parnell, a working couple in their fifties whose children had grown up and left home, took to Naomi, fussed over her broken leg, insisted they all have dinner with them and finally decided to buy a dog so

Naomi could come over after school and take it for a walk as 'punishment'.

By the time the discussion on what type of dog had finished, it was too late even for a cup of coffee. Anna, who was driving because it was easier for Naomi to get in and out of her car with her cast and crutches, offered to drop Pete back at the hospital where he'd left his car, before taking the child back to her parents.

'And leave you to face whatever consequences this new brainwave might incur?' he growled, pleased by the outcome of the meeting but smarting over having to share Anna with so many others—and having to forego the fantasy dinner he'd created in his mind.

'I don't think Mum will mind about the dog, although she's always said I can't have one,' Naomi answered, picking up on his meaning in spite of the careful selection of words. 'They were nice people, weren't they?'

'They were,' he agreed, after one glance at Anna's tight face told him she was making nasty comparisons between the couple and the parents of the child.

'You can't change people,' he told her later as they drove away after an icy reception at the Wilson household. 'All you can do is be there for Naomi if she needs you, and she knows that. You've already established yourself and the kids as friends. She doesn't live so far from you that she can't use your house as a refuge.'

'I thought you were against my befriending patients,' she snapped at him, shocking him by the shortness of the words.

'Well, I was, but that's for your sake. The job is demanding enough without all the emotional stuff that comes with it, and you look tired. I worry about you.'

He spoke gently but could see she wasn't appeased. If anything, she looked even grumpier.

'Well, don't! I'm not tired because I follow up on patients,' she told him. 'I'm tired because I can't sleep.'

Join the club, he wanted to say, but if he admitted to his insomnia problems she might ask him why, and he could hardly admit that tantalising images of her naked body, dancing through his dreams, had destroyed all chance of a good night's rest.

Asked her why instead, and got a glare for his trouble. Hadn't seen her glare much before tonight. Maybe he could introduce a glaring Anna to his subconscious and his dreams would return to normal.

Then he remembered how he pictured her naked and decided he'd stick with lack of sleep for a while, thought of the real thing, glanced her way and mentally stripped off her sensible blouse, remembered her in the black dress—wondered why she'd stopped the car.

'We're here,' she told him, but he was too lost in his dream to understand where 'here' was.

'Hospital car park—your car,' she added helpfully. 'Or would you like me to drive you home?'

'No, this is fine,' he assured her, turning towards her and seeing how close her lips were in the confines of her small vehicle. Remembered how they'd felt in the stairwell that night, wondered if they felt the same, if she tasted the same—

Moved towards her then remembered her confession. The words sounded in his head like a bad line from a Victorian melodrama. I love another!

Opened the car door and put one foot out onto firm ground.

'I'm selling kisses at the fête on Saturday,' he heard himself say. 'That's how I'm raising money. We all are, twelve of us—men, not women. It's equality, you see—political correctness and all that.'

Then he followed his foot out of the car, shut the door and staggered to his own car, fumbling in his pocket for the keys, wondering how he'd contrived to make such a mess of an evening which only yesterday had promised so much.

CHAPTER TEN

ANNA looked less tired next day, seemed quite chirpy, in fact, humming to herself and smiling when she didn't think Pete was watching her. Made him so suspicious he had to talk to David, carefully edging the conversation around to the state of his marriage.

'Thinking of dipping your toe into matrimonial waters at long last?' David asked him. 'Is that the explanation for this quiz?'

Pete protested, but David only laughed.

'Sally saw it coming. She said Anna would be the one to finally convince you the single life wasn't all it's cracked up to be.'

'Sally? Anna? What on earth do you mean?' David looked puzzled.

'It's not Anna?' he queried. 'Gosh, I'm sorry. Did I put my foot in it? I just thought— Well, I see you hanging around her, following her to meetings, always grabbing the chair beside her. I thought, well, you know, that there might be more than professional relationship between you.'

'Well, there isn't,' Pete told him, groaning inwardly as he realised what a fool he'd been making of himself. 'You're imagining things.'

'Me and half the hospital,' David responded gleefully. 'But if you say it's not then that's the end of it. In fact, I'll be glad to tell Sally she's wrong. She's so damned convinced about this feminine intuition stuff—reckoned she could tell how Anna felt about you from one glance. Pity, really, because she's a fine woman from what I've seen and heard of her. Good at her job but with a heart. Always helps in medicine. Keeps you human.'

Pete slouched away from Outpatients more confused than ever. Sally thought Anna was attracted to him?

No, David had got that wrong. Liz was a woman and she hadn't noticed it. Wondered if he should ask Kelly out just to get things back on an even keel. Decided he'd rather be celibate for the rest of his life than go back to that 'casual affair' stuff again.

Saw Anna greet another patient and knew celibacy was a bad option.

He realised he had absolutely no idea what to do—whom to ask—how to tackle it—so he drifted through to the end of his working week, seeing patients, admitting or dismissing them, working by rote, medicine by numbers, while Anna smiled her secret smile and hummed.

The fête began at ten. Ten until three the official hours, but most people came early. He saw Josh and Jackie several times, put up with their teasing and informed them his lips would only be on duty for an hour—between one and two.

'Do you charge by the second or the minute?' Josh asked, and Pete recoiled in mock horror.

'Kiss someone with that hair? I'd rather die!'

'It's for a good cause,' Josh reminded him. 'You could kiss me on the cheek.'

Jackie looked at him and blushed, then said shyly, 'I'm keeping five dollars. Will that be enough?'

How the hell had he got into this? He touched her on the shoulder.

'More than enough, my sweet,' he said. 'You, I'd kiss for nothing!'

She blushed again, muttered something about raising more money and dashed off through the crowd.

'She's very young for her age,' Josh said in a brotherly fashion. Then he glanced at Pete. 'How did you feel about boys kissing your sisters—when you were my age, I mean?'

Knew exactly what he meant. Answered honestly.

'With two of my sisters, the older ones, it didn't bother me. In fact, I guess I figured no one would ever want to kiss the eldest. She was a swat—brilliant, in fact. So somehow I thought she was exempt. I was absolutely stunned when she got engaged and married—even then I thought she and Rod probably discussed calculus instead of having sex, but they've produced three children so calculus must have something going for it.'

Josh chuckled, then waited hopefully.

'With the sister nearest to me in age, I wanted to punch the guys. Really weird, it was. I mean, it wasn't as if I had a thing for her. We fought like cat and dog, yet I hated the thought of some boy touching her. Fortunately she left home, went to university down south, and when she wasn't there I didn't think about what might be happening so I survived my adolescence without any assault charges against me.'

Josh grinned at him.

'Maybe it's a good thing I'm going away to uni next year,' he said, then he clapped Pete on the back. 'Thanks—I was beginning to think I was abnormal but it's not the sort of thing I could bother Anna about.'

Which brought her naturally into the conversation.

'Is she here?' Pete asked.

'Yep, selling jam over the far side,' Josh told him. 'Said we could do whatever we liked as long as it didn't involve getting into trouble. I'm going up in the rescue helicopter later— boy, is it neat!'

They talked and walked, Pete wondering if he needed any jam, Josh oblivious to Pete's growing need to see his stepmother, unconcerned about anything beyond his pleasure in the day and a few man-talk things he wanted aired.

They parted near the helicopter pad but by the time Pete had walked back to the jam stall Anna was gone. He wandered through the growing crowds, searching for a glimpse of her, wishing he'd asked Josh what she was wearing, wondering if she'd gone home and not stayed for his part in the festivities.

She was wearing blue, he discovered later when, with all the other contestants in the Hospital Heart-throb competition, he was lined up behind a series of hospital sheets, brightly painted with Adonis-like bodies with holes for the contestants' heads cut at an uncomfortable, for him, height.

Even before he stuck his head into his hole he could see her approaching, the thin blue straps of the dress making her skin look very pale, probably making her eyes bluer if only he could see that far!

Ken Riddell had the job of spruiker and he was doing it well, encouraging all the woman at the fête to roll up and pay for a kiss.

'Come on, ladies,' he pleaded. 'Pay by the minute or the hour—just a peck or a good smooch—what's it worth to you? The man who raises the most money will be named Hospital Heart-throb of the Year so grab your favourite medico. We all know how good they are with their hands—let's see what they can do with lips.'

'Can we try now and pay later?' someone called, bringing gales of laughter from the gathering crowd.

'Whatever suits you,' Ken assured her. 'But you have to be honest about it. If he's a five, that's five dollars—a ten, ten dollars. How about it, girls? All these lads are clean, tested for disease, but just in case we're sticking to cheeks so you can give him a peck on his or have his warm lips press your cheek—pay your money and take your choice.'

It was a silly idea, Pete realised, but it was causing a bit of light-hearted fun and perhaps would add a few dollars to the overall result.

He saw the women approaching, tentatively at first, then with growing courage as others lined up in front of him. Wondered if anyone had ever died of embarrassment. If killing Margie—whose idea it had been to nominate him—would count as justifiable homicide, heard more laughter and saw Josh join his line.

'Family rates,' Josh was saying to Ken as the crowds applauded his bravery, but Pete's first customer had arrived, lips pursed ready for a quick peck on his cheek. He felt his embarrassment reach new heights, decided it was a ridiculous, silly idea—transmitting spit and diseases! At a hospital fête! Then remembered the rules—no lip contact. The kisses were platonic—that had been decided very early on!

A few more pecks on the cheek from totally unknown women, then Jackie arrived, still blushing, tilted her cheek for a peck so he gave her two—one on each cheek. Josh next, kissing Pete on the cheek instead of vice versa—nice that he could kiss a man without feeling embarrassed—then the end of the 'family rates'—Anna.

Thought his heart would burst when he saw the glow in her eyes, the dimple dancing in her cheek.

'I've paid big money for this,' she said demurely, then she reached up and kissed him on the lips. He tried to grab her, to hold her to him, but the sheet was in the way, he couldn't get enough slack, realised he didn't need to hold her. She wasn't going anywhere.

Mouth to mouth they stood and kissed, no body contact at all—look, Mum, no hands. Felt the happiness slice through him, painful, uncertain, inexplicable—joy for sure—but so many questions. Realised people were cheering, shouting, yelling at something or someone, wondered how his legs were still supporting him as they went boneless with desire.

'I love you, Anna Crane,' he whispered as a realisation that the noise was directed at them made him break the contact.

Saw shock glaze her eyes.

'Do you expect to be paid extra for smart comments?' she snapped, and strode away, her rigid backbone declaring her displeasure for all to see.

He stared out through the sheet, saw people on his queue turn to watch Anna go, guessed what they must be thinking.

'I'll have what she had,' a pert voice said, and he realised he had a customer—Kelly.

He smiled at her, let her kiss him on the lips, wondered why one kiss could make his blood sing while another did no more than warm his lips. Somehow he made it through the session, nursing staff and patients both paying to peck his cheek and tease him a little about the Heart-throb tag.

Some Heart-throb! He'd finally found the one woman he wanted in his life—the for-ever-after woman—and had made a botch of things.

Or had he?

Was this all still connected with some 'un-attainable' man she fancied she loved? Damn it all, if she loved someone else, no matter how unattainable the joker was, how could she kiss him as she had?

Passionately!

With so much feeling his head had spun!

Or had he imagined it?

Had it all been one-sided?

His side?

Hell!

Remembered the advice he'd given Josh about women—open lines of communication, let them talk, listen to them.

Headed for the jam stall, hoping she might be back there, but all the products had been sold and the stall itself had been packed away. He found Jackie a little further on, haggling over the price of goldfish.

'Is Anna still here?' he demanded.

Saw a hurt expression in her eyes and realised she was holding up the bag of water so he could admire the fish she'd selected. He politely praised the fish, which looked particularly ordinary to him, and asked again.

'She must be because we're all going home together. Meeting at the car, which is in her usual parking place, at three if we get separated.'

He excused himself and plunged into the crowds again. Ran into Tim and Janice, hand in hand, the infamous dog—a vicious-looking bull-terrier—held on a short leash. He remem-

bered his manners this time, said hello and en-
quired about Mrs Jennings, before asking his
question.

The dog was licking at his shoes, its tail
wagging happily as if it might later work up
to a full meal—ankles, calves, knees, thighs.

'He's harmless,' Tim assured him. 'We
were playing rough when he bit me—it was
my fault. And he's great with Janice—
wouldn't let anyone touch her.'

He looked as fierce as the dog when he said
this and Pete smiled. Maybe this was one love
story which would have a happy ending.

Met another partially happy ending next.
Naomi on crutches, Mr and Mrs Parnell walking slowly alongside her, a small bundle of
white fur stumbling around their feet.

'We were a bit like the Wilsons,' Mr Parnell
admitted, drawing him aside while Mrs Parnell
helped Naomi choose a pendant for her
mother. 'Too busy making money to spend
time with the children as they grew up. It
worked out all right for us, but this business
brought home how lucky we were. We're
pleased to be helping out with her.'

He asked if they'd seen Anna, was met by regrets and head-shaking and walked on, wondering if she might be in the tea tent. He was caught by Margie for a while, teased about the kisses, but still no Anna. The crowds were thinning, people drifting away, stalls being folded to be put away until next year. Then, across the heads, he saw a tall familiar figure.

What the hell was Callum doing here?

He hurried towards him and found the object of his search attached quite firmly to Callum's arm.

Felt his heart stop beating, a dozen swear words ricochet through his mind. It couldn't be Callum she loved. Not his brother! His very-married brother!

'Hi, Pete.'

She greeted him as if the kiss—and his declaration—had never happened. Her eyes were glowing with the excitement he'd seen earlier—and stupidly imagined was for him. She'd known Callum was coming—she'd been all aglow for him!

Swore again internally—and tried to catch up on the conversation.

'I don't know why I hadn't figured out you were brothers—I mean, seeing you together, there is a resemblance, and although I knew you had a big family I just didn't make the connection. Guess I've always thought of Callum by his first name, not considered the Dr Jackson bit.'

She was talking too much, a sure sign, he'd discovered, that she was more rattled than she let on. Why?

He scowled at his brother.

'Well, I'm pleased to see you, too,' Callum said, clapping his arms around Pete's shoulders and giving him a hug. 'Had a bad day? Anna was telling me about the Heart-throb business—must have been hell for someone like you!'

Pete glanced at Anna to see how she'd taken the tired family joke of him as a Don Juan.

Was sorry he'd glanced that way for he caught a hint of sadness in her eyes—wanted to hold and comfort her, to tell her the pain would eventually go away, although he wasn't certain his would.

Ever.

'I was looking for you,' he said instead. 'I thought we might grab a bite to eat together tonight.' That was good—keep it casual. 'Make up for the meal we missed the other day.'

Callum was tapping him on the shoulder and he realised he hadn't asked why Callum was here. Decided he didn't want to know but he faced his brother anyway.

'Aren't you forgetting something?' Callum asked.

Pete shook his head.

'What kind of something?'

Callum sighed and muttered to no one in particular, 'He's got it bad.' Then he said, 'Why would I be here? At your hospital fête? Isn't that stretching brotherly support just a little far? What's the date, bonehead?'

Pete tried to think. He remembered getting an invitation a month or so ago and thinking it was for the same date as the hospital fête.

'Oh, no! Jason's back! It's Liz's engagement party. Are you the only family coming? Or did I tell Mum and Dad they could stay with me?' Hit his forehead with his palm. 'I've been so darned busy I've forgotten what we arranged. Hell!'

Carefully, Callum explained the arrangements. Yes, his parents were staying at Pete's place and, having declined to join Callum at the fête, were probably already settling into his spare bedroom. Jill was also here with her family, staying at the same hotel as Callum and his wife, and currently organising babysitters through the hotel for all the children.

'Do you want to know the place and time?' he added with a grin.

'At the Garden Palace, eight o'clock,' Pete muttered, finally putting all the missing pieces into place. He glanced towards Anna, who was looking more and more forlorn, and said hopefully, 'It will still be a bite to eat, and you know Liz already—would you like to come?'

She shook her head.

'I can't intrude on a private party,' she objected.

He glanced from her to Callum and wondered if that was why she didn't want to join them. Felt more confused than ever, especially when Callum started persuading her, telling her how pleased Caroline, his wife, would be to see her.

'She's missed having you around to exchange female doctor stuff with,' he said, 'especially now she's stopped work to mind the kids and misses all the gossip.'

Saw Anna's pleasure at the remark and decided perhaps it wasn't Callum she loved after all. Remembered Anna had been in Huntley for four years—surely unrequited passion couldn't last that long.

Remembered passion in the kiss and wondered if he was losing his mind.

Definitely losing track of conversations. It seemed as if Anna had agreed to attend the party.

With him?

It was with him. Once he'd figured that out, he stumbled through the practical arrangements of transport and agreed to collect her at a quarter to eight.

She wandered off, still attached to Callum's arm, while he debated whether to follow them and snatch her away onto *his* arm or to dance a small jig to release some of the happiness inside him. Though why he should be happy because she'd agreed to go to Liz's party, he couldn't say. Perhaps half a loaf was better than nothing.

Anna was wearing white—virginal. A simple kind of suit arrangement with a soft, swirly skirt reaching to her knees and a fitted jacket in heavier material. Her hair, caught back as it had been when she'd modelled at the cocktail party, frothed about her head. She looked beautiful and he said so, bringing perplexity into her eyes.

They said goodbye to Josh and Jackie and walked out to the front verandah, where she paused.

'Forget something?' he asked.

She looked into his eyes, her own face lit by the outside light left burning at night. Shook her head and then, in what he was beginning to realise was typically Anna-fashion, asked the million dollar question.

'What did you mean when you said you loved me?' Paused as if not certain he'd remember saying it. 'At the fête. After we kissed?'

'What do you mean, what did I mean?' he demanded, his heart thudding so hard against his chest he felt ill. 'Wasn't it clear enough?'

She half smiled and once again her head waggled from side to side.

'Not from you—the non-matrimonial type,' she said softly. 'You know my situation—my responsibilities. I couldn't have an affair with you, Pete. What kind of an example would that be for two teenagers? And what about you? The man who doesn't want to be tied down? A wife might be a tie, but a ready-made family? That's more than a tie—it's shackles, balls and chains, the whole bit. It would be too much for you to take on.'

'It wasn't for you,' he argued, and the smile grew—a trifle misty but the full tilt of lips.

'Ah, but that was different,' she said. 'I loved Ted, loved them all. I'd felt that way for years. Marrying him was simply an extension of that love, plus it gave me legal right to make decisions for him—for all of them.'

He reached out and touched her cheek as a new solution occurred to him. Wondered if he could compete with a ghost.

'Do you still love him?' he asked. 'Is he the unattainable man you spoke of?'

She looked puzzled, then surprised, then she chuckled and leaned forward, kissing him lightly on the lips.

'No, that was you, stupid,' she said softly, then led the way down the steps and out towards his car while he stared after her, totally bewildered. 'You gave me the ''look but don't touch'' message right from the start.'

Eventually he followed her, made it to the driver's seat, started the engine, went backwards instead of forwards this time, and began the drive to the centre of town, his head whirling.

'If you love me and I love you, what's the problem?' he said, when his thoughts had finally sorted themselves into a coherent question.

'It's all the other stuff,' she said, fluttering her hands as if to encompass problems of enormous import. 'About marriage and commitment and that for-ever-after business. I don't know if I'm cut out for it—I think I've probably dodged thinking about it by marrying friends instead of lovers.'

Relief surged through him. It was herself she doubted, not him.

'We'll sort it out, won't hurry things,' he promised, and felt her tremble as he slid his finger up the inside of her arm, his body responding to that slight movement with a sudden urgency.

Then realised she was laughing.

'Oh, I wouldn't bet on that,' she said dryly. 'In fact, it's my guess you're already debating how quickly you can get me into bed.'

He had been, but that was different. Besides, he was a man and it was natural for men to think that way—wasn't it?

'I was talking about not hurrying the marriage part,' he muttered, then a lot of things clicked into place in his mind, clues he'd been given which might explain her attitude. He pulled over to the side of the road and stopped the car.

'How did you end up in a foster-home?' he asked, taking her hand and holding it in his, silently telling her he was ready to listen, praying that she'd talk to him—sex forgotten as he realised how very much he loved her.

Anna sighed and bent her head, teased her thumb across his palm.

'I didn't know my father. My mother never spoke of him, but the man who lived with her, my stepfather, made very sure I knew I wasn't his.'

He heard the pain of that childhood rejection in her voice and his heart ached for her.

'He abused her, abused us both, not physically but verbally. All the time. Shouting at us for minor misdemeanours, quietly scathing when the sin was greater. From when I was old enough to realise she was desperately unhappy, I tried to persuade my mother to leave him. For two years I plotted and planned, worked out ways we could get away, went to her with ideas, but, like Mrs Jennings, she refused to leave—said he'd never hurt her so what excuse could she give?'

She reclaimed her hand and wrapped her arms around her shoulders as if suddenly very cold.

'When I was twelve I stole money from his wallet and went myself. I ran away. He reported the theft, said I'd already left home and had broken in to steal the money. He told the authorities I was no good, that he'd done all he could and that he wanted nothing more to do with me. The police found me, of course. I had no idea where to go or what to do so I was wandering around the city. I was put into temporary care then taken to the children's court. No one told me why my mother didn't come to see me, not until the social workers came to take me to my first foster-home. They told me she'd taken an overdose the night I ran away—that she'd been in a coma for four days before she died.'

Pete gathered her in his arms and held her, feeling a grief too deep for tears juddering in her body.

'It would have happened some time if she was so desperately unhappy that she took her own life,' he suggested, wondering how often she must have said the words to herself.

'Not if I'd stayed,' she whispered. 'While I was there she had to stay alive to be there for me.'

'But was she?' he asked. 'Wouldn't she have left if she'd really cared for you? Have you never asked yourself if perhaps she accepted his abuse as a form of love?'

She moved, pushing herself away from him.

'Yes, often,' she admitted. 'And now I understand a little more about mental illness and realise that's what she suffered, why she needed the pills she took, I know it was probably inevitable. I've also learnt a lot about her childhood, the abuse she'd suffered. A man who didn't physically hurt her must have seemed like salvation.'

'And you? How has that abuse, your random childhood in foster-homes, affected you, apart from what I know—that you give and give and give all you can, leaving little of your energy for Anna.'

Once again she looked into his eyes.

'I don't know,' she said honestly. 'That's why I'm so wary. What if something terrible comes out in me? What if I'm not capable of forming a normal relationship?'

He grinned at her.

'Well, you've got the same doubts about me,' he teased, 'so maybe we're a good match.'

He started the engine and drove on, more at ease now although nothing had been resolved.

His family closed ranks around her, taking her into their midst as if she was someone very special to them. Exactly how he hoped she'd be—eventually.

'No, Mum, no wedding bells,' he told his mother when she asked a few pertinent questions later. 'Not yet at least. Not until we both know how far we can push the boundaries of our privacy—until we find out where a relationship between us will lead. We're going to take this very slowly.'

'Well, you know best,' his mother told him, but he didn't like the way she smiled at him—

as if she knew far more about him than he knew himself.

And when he danced with Anna later, his body rampant in its desire for her, physical hunger straining at his skin, he reconsidered the 'slowly'. Wondered how he was going to keep his hands off her at work. In front of Josh and Jackie. How he'd got himself into this mess!

'You're sure about the affair?' he asked when he drove her home, much later, and knew he wanted more than just an unsatisfactory kiss in the front seat of the car.

She shrugged.

'I'm not sure about anything any more,' she admitted, and he felt a whoop of joy inside himself, then a squelch of reality as he realised she'd made it harder, not easier, handing the responsibility to him like that. Responsibility for someone else's happiness—three someone elses probably—was a very scary thought. Dampening as well.

He took her in his arms and kissed her gently, curbing the passion, hiding his fiery need, not wanting to frighten her.

But her own fire tempted him, taunted him, danced along his nerves so he responded more strongly than he'd intended—kissing her lips, her eyelids, her chin, his hands moving on her breasts, slipping under the jacket to feel their heaviness, wondering if she wanted him as badly as he wanted her, if women felt arousal deep in their bellies, felt the heat of it thundering in their blood.

Pushed himself away eventually, breathing deeply, afraid the sexual aspect of this new type of relationship might mess things up before it had a firm basis. Move slowly, keep it casual, he reminded himself.

'Let's go for a drive tomorrow—all four of us, if the kids would like to come. I'll phone Liz and get her to pack a picnic.'

Anna chuckled, the low sound brushing against his eardrums like a melody.

'You have your parents staying with you and I'm sure they expect to see something of you tomorrow, and I doubt very much that Liz will want to get up at the crack of dawn to pack a picnic basket for you. It was her party, remember, and she was still dancing when we left.'

'How can you be so sensible at a time like this?' he grouched. 'And my parents will leave by lunchtime to drive home. May I visit in the afternoon, please, ma'am?'

She touched his cheek and ran a hand through his hair, exactly as he'd seen her do with Josh. Only he doubted that Josh reacted the same way he did.

'Come late afternoon and stay for tea,' she suggested. 'And Trivial Pursuit. If you're game, take on Josh.'

He had to be content with that, to move slowly, give her time and space—think ahead himself about how he'd cope as a stepfather to those teenagers, how they'd feel about accepting him, if it was really what he wanted—for for-ever-after!

CHAPTER ELEVEN

SLOWLY! It became the key word in their progress, although there was nothing slow about the way Pete's heart raced when he saw Anna for the first time each morning or came across her unexpectedly during the day.

Nothing slow about her kisses either, which were hot with a passion he could feel building inside her, meeting his and matching it, smouldering just below the surface as they paced themselves and tried to think with their heads, not their hearts and loins.

He made it through one week, then almost two, but by Friday afternoon of the second week he was so frustrated he spent the day snapping at the staff, particularly Anna, who countered by snapping back at him.

Caught her in the office late in the afternoon, slammed the door shut and took her in his arms.

276

'I can't go on like this!' he muttered against her hair when he'd kissed her thoroughly and had her held hard against his straining body.

'Me neither,' she mumbled back at him, then she raised her face to look at him, her eyes scanning his face as if trying to read something in it. 'I'll do something about it,' she promised. 'It's a quiet afternoon—may I have an early mark?'

He nodded, too bemused to argue.

'Will I see you later?' he asked, wondering if the invitation to dinner which had been forthcoming every night since the engagement party would be issued.

She grinned at him.

'You go home when you finish work,' she suggested. 'I'll contact you there.'

Which she did, only not by phone—in person. Three hours later, turning up on his doorstep with a small bag clutched in her hand and a terrified expression on her face.

He nodded towards the bag.

'Going out later to do a spot of burglary?' he asked.

Got a sick smile in reply.

'I—I've come to stay,' she stammered. 'That's if you want me to, if you think it's OK, if it's all right with you. For the night, that kind of stay, with you, in bed...'

She lost it then, her voice disappearing completely, swallowed up by the embarrassment which had made her cheeks go as bright a red as her hair.

Not that he was faring much better. He was too stunned to react so he stood and stared at her.

'You could ask me in,' she suggested eventually. 'Or tell me to go away.'

'No!'

Didn't know if he said that aloud or not, but at least the word shocked him into action. He took her hand and led her in, went back and shut the door—back again and locked it—then returned to take her in his arms. Holding her close, he guided her to a chair, then sat down and pulled her onto his knee, unwilling to be parted from her, wanting her weight pressing down on him.

'Why now?' he asked, and saw her smile, knew everything was going to be all right as his heart leapt about in his chest and his own smile answered hers.

She took a deep breath then turned to him, studying him in that direct way she had.

'I talked to the kids about it,' she said. 'It seemed the best thing to do under the circumstances.' Now his heart began palpitating! She'd discussed their sex life—or potential sex life—with two teenagers? 'I told them how I felt about you, how I really wanted to experience a physical relationship with you but I was worried how they might feel about it if it didn't work out between us. Would they think less of me? Be disappointed in me? Feel I'd betrayed them in any way or set a bad example for them?'

Now he was over the shock he was awed—overawed, in fact! Couldn't imagine the courage it had taken for her to speak to them that way.

'And?' he prompted, wrapping his arms more tightly around her.

She smiled and kissed him on the lips.

'Jackie packed my bag and Josh gave me a talk on safe sex then produced a condom he swore was handed out at school when they had health education lectures.'

Pete bowed his head and rested it on her shoulder, feeling a prick of tears in his eyes as he realised the boundless love this woman spun around her, feeling humble that he was included in its web.

'They said they'd order pizza for dinner on Sunday and would we please be home by six as we'd promised a championship game of you-know-what.'

'You're mine for the whole weekend?' he asked, trembling with the enormity of this move on her part.

'For ever, I think!' she said shakily. 'Depending, of course, on how this sex business pans out.'

He smiled and held her, sex giving way to love, his heart too full to speak, to do anything more than hold her.

'Well, are you compatible?' Josh asked when they walked into the big house, hand in hand on Sunday afternoon.

'I think we could make do,' Pete said, wondering why he wasn't more embarrassed by the lad's question, realising it was because it had been asked with affection, not prurient interest.

Anna, on the other hand, had blushed scarlet and disappeared, mumbling something about putting her clothes away. She'd blushed when he'd undressed her, as they'd made love, when he'd looked into her eyes afterwards and told her how much he loved her, worshipped her, wanted her for his wife.

Josh put out his hand.

'I'm really glad for both of you, and so's Jackie,' he said gruffly. 'We had a talk and she wanted me to say that if ever you feel we're in the way, please, just say so.'

Pete felt a thickening in his throat and wondered if love made all men sentimental.

'I'm sure you'd never get in the way,' he responded, clapping this full-grown would-be 'son' on the shoulder. 'What I'd like to say to you is that I don't want to intrude into your space or into parts of your life where you don't want me. Will you tell me if I upset you? If anything I do aggravates you?'

'You're worrying about Dad,' Josh said with a maturity that surprised Pete. 'Well, don't. He was Dad, and you're Pete. We only shared this house with him for holidays and then for that last year when he was really sick. Anna set his bed up here in the living room so he could be part of the household, not shut away in a bedroom. I sleep in the room he and Mum used on holidays so if you want to come and live here with us, which we'd really like, you won't have Dad's ghost following you around.'

Pete sighed and cuffed him again on the shoulder.

'And when did you get so clever?' he asked. 'I thought I was the one who was supposed to be dealing out the adult wisdom.'

Josh grinned at him.

'I did enjoy our little man-to-man talks but I have to admit, once Jackie and I figured out you were the one Anna was interested in, we decided I'd better spend a bit of time with you, get to know you, check you out, before she got too deeply into something, like!'

'I can't believe this!' Pete complained. 'When you two figured out—? I thought I was running this courtship, not you.'

'Does it matter who was running it as long as it all turned out right in the end?' Jackie demanded, entering the room in time to hear the end of the conversation. 'And the two of you can live happily together for-ever-after?'

'I don't suppose so,' Pete admitted, looking up as Anna joined them, a faint flush lingering on her cheeks and stars dancing in her eyes.

Funny that, seeing stars in the sky during daytime!

MEDICAL ROMANCE™

Large Print

Titles for the next six months...

February

ONE IN A MILLION	Margaret Barker
POLICE SURGEON	Abigail Gordon
IZZIE'S CHOICE	Maggie Kingsley
THE HUSBAND SHE NEEDS	Jennifer Taylor

March

HER PASSION FOR DR JONES	Lilian Darcy
BACHELOR CURE	Marion Lennox
HOLDING THE BABY	Laura MacDonald
SEVENTH DAUGHTER	Gill Sanderson

April

PRACTICALLY PERFECT	Caroline Anderson
TAKE TWO BABIES...	Josie Metcalfe
TENDER LIAISON	Joanna Neil
A HUGS-AND-KISSES FAMILY	Meredith Webber

MILLS & BOON®

Makes any time special™

MEDICAL ROMANCE™

Large Print

May

A FAMILIAR FEELING	Margaret Barker
HEART IN HIDING	Jean Evans
HIS MADE-TO-ORDER BRIDE	Jessica Matthews
A TIMELY AFFAIR	Helen Shelton

June

THE COURAGE TO SAY YES	Lilian Darcy
DOCTORS IN CONFLICT	Drusilla Douglas
THE PERFECT TREATMENT	Rebecca Lang
PERFECT TIMING	Alison Roberts

July

VETS AT CROSS PURPOSES	Mary Bowring
A MILLENNIUM MIRACLE	Josie Metcalfe
A CHANGE OF HEART	Alison Roberts
HEAVEN SENT	Carol Wood

MILLS & BOON®

Makes any time special™